CATERPILLAR HALL

Caterpillar Hall

By

ANNE BARRETT

With drawings by

CATHERINE CUMMINS

COLLINS
ST. JAMES'S PLACE LONDON
1950

PRINTED IN GREAT BRITAIN
COLLINS CLEAR-TYPE PRESS : LONDON AND GLASGOW
1950

MJ

TO
THORNHILL

WITH LOVE

Contents

8 *Contents*

Illustrations

CHAPTER I

A Very Special Sort of Present

"An umbrella, please," said Penelope.

"But, dear," said Miss Pink, "I don't think you quite understand. This is a very special sort of present. I've never known a little girl of your age be sent so much money to spend. Five whole pounds! Now I'd have said get some nice little thing and put the rest in Savings, but your father writes specially to say you're to have it all and get something you really want. Now think again, dear."

" I really want an umbrella, please," said Penelope.

" Penelope ! " Miss Pink was getting flustered. " Think, child ! You could have anything ; one of those lovely sleeping dolls at Hamleys, or a workbox lined with satin, or—or even a new bicycle, or . . ." Her imagination, never very strong, was beginning to fail her.

" I don't like dolls any more and I've got a work-box and my old bicycle's quite good enough, so please may I have an umbrella ? " Penelope thought this all very tiresome when all she wanted to do was to be off and start buying it. After all, her father had said to get what she wanted, and this was it. Why should she get what someone else, and Miss Pink at that, thought she ought to want?

Miss Pink's little mouth was pursed up in distress. " But *why* an umbrella, dear ? " she asked. " There are lots in the hall you could borrow and you know you always have your sou'wester when it rains. It's most unsuitable for a child ; it really is. I'm sure that wasn't your father's idea at all."

Penelope wriggled angrily. How dare Miss Pink pretend to know what her father's ideas were ! Certainly he'd understand when she wrote, and send back one of his own lovely letters from Persia, saying, " Of course, my darling, the only thing to get. How wise you are." She went off into a daydream of the time when he would come back and all life would be like that, till the realisation that Miss Pink was still talking brought her back again.

" But *why* an umbrella, dear ? If you could only explain. . . ."

Penelope wriggled again. How could she explain what she felt about umbrellas to Miss Pink ? How could she make her understand the wonderful privateness of being under your own little green tent roof, for it must be green ? How the handle would be your own little tree with spreading branches, a palmy oasis in some desolate desert, so that whenever you put up your umbrella in the park or in the road you would suddenly be an explorer, secret and alone, under your own tropical sky. How the rain might beat, and you be snug beneath ; or how, once it was up, you might be clinging to a parachute, journeying upwards to the moon. Oh, and such a host of other things too ! How could she tell her the endless fascination of the taut, squeaky noise they made when you first put them up and opened out the shining silk, or the pippy, seedy rattle they made when the hard rain came squelching down on them. How could she tell her the enchantment of the little spoke-ends that stuck out all round, so small and entrancing ? It was no use trying, even if she'd wanted to.

" I just want one, Miss Pink. A green one."

" Well, it's really *too* tiresome of you, Penelope, I didn't think you could ever be so silly ! I shall have to ask your Uncle Everard to see you, because I really don't like to do such a foolish thing on my own responsibility. Five pounds ! And all you can think of is an umbrella ! " and she clucked and bridled out of the room.

Penelope sighed. Why did Miss Pink get so agitated about everything that didn't matter, and then be as dull as she could be when something really exciting happened ? And why couldn't she understand that those dingy old black cotton umbrellas in the hall wouldn't be the same thing at all. Ugh ! The very thought of them put her teeth on edge.

She went to the window of her room and knelt on the cushioned seat, looking out over the Square gardens. The leaves of the plane trees had turned golden brown and were circling down, leaving only the bare strings of bobbles swinging on the branches. Between the leafless greeny-grey splotched trunks the houses on the opposite side of the Square, with their stone porticos, were easy to see.

She'd been in London for two years now, ever since Daddy had gone to Persia, and was living with his brother, Uncle Everard ; Miss Pink, her governess ; and Prewitt and Mrs. Prewitt in the kitchen.

Darling Prewitts ! thought Penelope ; somehow when you thought about them it made you feel as if you were near a warm fire, while being with Miss Pink was like . . . what was it like exactly ? Oh, yes, she knew ; one of those showers of April rain when the sun ought to be out. And being with Uncle Everard . . . well, she did love him in a sort of way, and she wanted terribly to see him smile and be happy, but oh dear, it was rather like a misty October afternoon when you couldn't see anything very clearly. And Daddy ? Oh, that was the wind blowing and cuckoos shouting and clouds racing above the downs by Seventrees.

Seventrees ! They'd only been there once, on a lovely boisterous April day. They had driven out from their rooms in Bidmouth and were standing on the downs, looking down at the house.

"There it is, Penelope," her father had said, "there's our home. But it's been let to strangers ever since Everard and I were boys, and that's why I must go abroad and leave you, darling, so that I can make enough money for us all to live there. God grant it won't take too long."

Penelope looked down at the house with its smooth lawns and walled gardens, sheltered by grey-trunked beeches, and it looked so dear and friendly and gracious that she immediately felt a great rush of love for it. Then out of the house came a little ant, a man, and stood on the lawn looking across the fields as though he owned them. She clutched her father's hand and looked at him, and as they both looked in each other's eyes, they realised that they were feeling exactly the same thing.

"It's *our* house," she said fiercely. "Yes, I understand, Daddy." And she put off thinking

" There it is, Penelope "

about the time when he must go so that they could enjoy the rest of that glorious day.

And how they did ! They trespassed in the woods and picnicked there and stalked the tenant through the edge of his own garden so that they could look in at the windows. They skirted round by the cottage where the Prewitts used to live and left all sorts of secret marks to recognise when they should come back. As a last solemn rite they picked up a beechnut husk from the crunchy, masty ground beneath the trees and split it in two to keep a half each. And from then onwards Seventrees had become the warm and dear background of all Penelope's dreams.

" Why Seven, Daddy ? " she had asked on the tired and happy way home, " there must be hundreds and hundreds of trees."

" I think it's the old name of the hill up behind," her father had replied, " but ask your Uncle Everard, he knows everything there is to know about the place."

And now it had happened, Daddy was gone and had been gone two years. Penelope climbed down from the window-seat and went to the little box where she kept the beechnut husk. She held it

to her forehead and for a moment was under the
trees, hearing the wind sigh through them ; then
she kissed it and put it back again. She'd learnt
not to try and make that particular magic work
for more than a second, for otherwise it would be
like when you smelt all the smell out of a rose so
that there was none left. Then she thought she'd
go and see the Prewitts, as Miss Pink would be
safely out of the way for a few minutes, changing
her book at the Library.

Down below she found Mrs. Prewitt ironing,
with a nice comfortable smell of not-quite-scorching
and a snowy, shiny pile of handkerchiefs mounting
up on the table. Prewitt, in a leather apron, was
polishing silver and making his own nice pink
powdery and methylated smell. They always had
lovely smells about them, the Prewitts.

Penelope told them her exciting new discovery
about people's weathers. ". . . and you're a cosy
evening with a fire, and Christmas coming near,"
she said, " and Miss Pink's a thin sort of miserable
spring rain that never stops."

" Lor' bless the child ! " exclaimed Mrs. Prewitt,
slapping down the iron and skating it to and fro.
" You mustn't say things like that ! " William

Prewitt gave a chuckle, being very much in agreement as to the shower-like qualities of Miss Pink. " And what do you reckon your own weather is, lovey ? " she went on.

" Five o'clock in the marnin', whatever time o' year it was, that's what I'd say," said William. " A fine noise goin' on, cocks crowin' and birds shoutin' and . . ."

" Are you there, Penelope ? " Miss Pink's thin little nose looked disapprovingly round the door. " Come along up now, dear, your Uncle Everard wishes to see you."

CHAPTER II

Uncle Everard

EVERARD PARFITT had just finished his tea when they went in, the dark-red curtains were drawn and the heavy silver teapot gleamed in the firelight. Penelope had only once been to a doctor in her life, but ever since then this room reminded her of the waiting-room she'd sat in that afternoon, everything was dark and heavy and shiny. Secretly Uncle Everard thought so too, but the house had been like that when he took it over, and he'd looked at it, and felt lost, and didn't know where to begin.

He lowered his *Times* and looked at them. " Ah, Penelope," he said vaguely, " yes, you'll be wanting that money your father sent for you. What a big present, and not even a birthday or a Christmas one, that's the best sort, isn't it ? Now you'll be sure and help her choose something really good, Miss Pink, won't you ? Something she really wants, nothing trumpery," and peeling off five clean new pound notes from a bundle in his pocket-book, he gave them to Penelope. " Run along now, my dear."

" But about the umbrella ? " flustered Miss Pink. " You said——"

" Well, it's a queer thing to think of, but is that what you really want, Penelope ? " As he looked at her closely for a moment out of his troubled, short-sighted eyes, Penelope suddenly thought to herself that he really was a bit like Daddy after all.

" Oh, yes ! It is," she said.

" Well, then, why not ? " he said, surprisingly. " The most important thing in life is to know what you want. Take her off to Hargroves to-morrow to get one, Miss Pink," and he turned back to the pages of *The Times*.

Miss Pink's mouth was pursing up again. " Oh, thank you, thank you, darling Uncle Everard ! " cried Penelope and dancing round to the back of his chair she hugged and kissed him.

" There, there," he said, pecking at her cheek in some embarrassment, " cut along now, dear," and waited to hear the door shut so that he could concentrate on the foreign news again. But oddly enough when she had gone the room seemed colder and he found he hadn't much heart for *The Times*. A feeling of discomfort filled him. Other people's children, he thought, other people's houses ; dealing with other people's lives. Even other people's adventures in the books he read ; in the paper. He wasn't all that old, younger than Charles, in fact, but where was his life ? Where had it gone to ? And as he had looked at his room, Everard Parfitt looked at his life for one chilly moment, and felt lost, and didn't know where to begin to put it right.

CHAPTER III

Joseph

PENELOPE woke up next morning to see a clear, deep-blue sky out of the window, and with a glorious feeling that something good was going to happen. The crisp sunlight shone through the bare trees and made flickery watery patches on the yellow walls. The air smelt of chrysanthemums and frost. The umbrella! They were going to Hargroves this very afternoon to buy it, and to-morrow—she hardly dared believe it, when she woke up, it would be standing there by the chair, beside her bed ! Of course, you wouldn't be able to open it indoors, but you'd be able to see the silk, and the knob of it and all the delicious little spokes, and as soon as breakfast was over you could run out into the Square. . . .

She jumped out of bed and pulled on her clothes, then she took down her father's photograph from the chest of drawers and kissed it so hard that afterwards she had to polish off the wet and sticky kiss-marks from the glass. She looked at the beech-nut husk to see if it were still safe in its box ; said " Seventrees " seven times to herself with great intensity, facing west, where Seventrees lay ; and then, as the last part of her morning's ritual, she looked at Great-great-aunt Prudence's sampler, which hung over her bed.

There, between the faded rows of little square, cross-stitch roses, she read :

> " *Yesterday returneth not,*
> *Perchance to-morrow cometh not,*
> *There is to-day—misuse it not.*"

and underneath, " Prudence Parfitt, 1826."

" Look at it every morning," her father had said, the very last night before he went away, " it used to be in the nursery at Seventrees when we were small, and it's the very best advice I ever had in my life."

Well, there wasn't any trouble about to-day's now.! Brimming with excitement and good resolutions, Penelope opened the door and ran out to wash, and then downstairs to breakfast.

She was so angelic at her lessons that morning that Miss Pink was quite surprised, but it all seemed so easy in that lovely frosty sunlight with the golden afternoon looming in front of her. And really Miss Pink wasn't such a bad old stick after all, in fact she supposed she wasn't really even very old ; she got quite flushed and excited when they were reading *Sir Patrick Spens* together, and it was all rather fun. They did apples, too, in Botany, and when Penelope felt that she couldn't bear for another moment to go on reading about the " sweet, white, juicy flesh," it made her so hungry, Miss Pink surprisingly gave her one to eat and took one herself.

Mrs. Prewitt had sent up Irish stew for lunch, which Penelope adored, and then that, too, was over and the glorious moment had come. They were standing on the front doorstep and then off on their way to Hargroves ! The air was keen and spicy with the mysterious smell of London in the autumn and as their bus swung down Park Lane there were blue misty distances between and beyond the leafless trees, full of promise and enchantment. At last they were really there, outside the heavy glass swing-doors, which a commissionaire was holding open for them.

" First floor ! " said an elegant blonde lady when Miss Pink asked the way. " Lifts to the right ! " and they plunged deeper and deeper into the fascinating cave of the shop, past flowers and stockings and foamy lace and the tropical scented air of the powder and perfume counter. It's like going past all the lands in the world quickly, thought Penelope as they caught a haunting whiff of cigars and cedarwood boxes that reminded her of Daddy.

" Here we are," said Miss Pink, and they were in a place that might have been in the middle of the earth, with rows of busy little miners' cages endlessly arriving and departing, green arrows up and red arrows down. They waited for a green arrow and then went shooting up at a speed that sent Penelope's tummy into her ankles.

" Umbrellas to the right ! " said the liftman as they got out, and they were there.

Penelope had never seen so many umbrellas in her life. They hung from the ceiling, sprouted from the ground and lay about in heaps on the tables. There were wide-open ones, like bright tropical birds in flight, bunches of flower-like ones half-open in gay umbrella-stands, dumpy, perky ones peeping everywhere, and, at the back, rows of stiff and sombre ones like people in church. They were checked and spotted and striped and flowered in all colours of the rainbow, and their handles were carved and contorted out of the most lovely and satisfying lumps of every sort of substance in the world, clear and grained and cloudy. But somehow Penelope was worried. They weren't *quite* right, there wasn't one that seemed to belong to her, they were *too* bright and new and shiny.

The assistant was holding up one after another, till she was quite bewildered, and Miss Pink, carried away in spite of herself, was squeaking and fluttering with excitement. " What about that one, dear, that's very handsome . . . or this . . .

She found him

Not too long a handle, of course, Miss . . ."
Penelope had wandered off and was looking at the
serious, sober ones in their slotted stands, feeling
rather sorry for them, when suddenly, leaning
rakishly at one end of a stand, she found him.

His head was cocked to one side and out of his
bright, beady, parrot's eye she could have sworn
that he winked at her. Beneath the delicately
carved head with its curving yellow beak was a
little gold ring and from that hung a magnificent
silken tassel with threads of every shade of blue and
green you could ever think of. The covering of
the umbrella itself was a rich shiny silk, just the
right shade of bluey-green for an intrepid explorer's
sky, and—wonder of wonders !—at the end of each
little spoke was a tiny ivory acorn, delicately and
wonderfully carved with miniature cup and fairy
fruit. Joseph, she thought she'd call him.

" This one, please," said Penelope, and handed
it to the assistant, who looked puzzled.

" Why, I've never seen that one before ! " she
exclaimed. " Where did you get it from ? "

Penelope showed her. " Well, all that lot are
a pound. I suppose it must have been reduced as
it's an old-fashioned style. But you're certainly

a clever girl to find it—just look at that silk. And I do declare that's a real gold band ! Well, you are lucky. Sort of knowing he looks, doesn't he ? " she said to Miss Pink.

" Well, I don't know that I'd have chosen quite such a striking head," said Miss Pink, beginning to purse a little as a matter of habit, " but still, the child must know her own mind."

" Oh, please, please, be quick ! " begged Penelope in an agony of impatience, and the girl, who was an understanding sort of person and remembered what she felt like as a child, hurried away with the umbrella and the bill.

Holding him lovingly and carefully in both hands, and tight against herself so that he shouldn't get squashed in the lift, Penelope went down again, and walked round in a happy dream, taking occasional peeps at him while Miss Pink hunted up and down counters for possible Christmas presents. As they came out into the street again it was dusk, the lamps were lit and glistened in a slight drizzle.

" Look, de " said Miss Pink, " isn't that exciting ? It's spotting now so you'll be able to christen your new umbrella."

" Oh, no ! " said Penelope. " I couldn't. . . . I mean . . . I haven't undone him properly yet . . . I want . . ." and gave up. Oh, she *couldn't* open Joseph with Miss Pink there, not for the lovely exciting first time, not ever, really, she thought. She'd want to come in under it too, or make silly remarks about it. Oh, no !

" Well, of all the tiresome, contrary children ! " exclaimed Miss Pink, who was very tired after all the shopping and poking round, and bundled her crossly on to a homeward bound bus.

CHAPTER IV

No Way Out of the Garden

PENELOPE was now considered old enough to go to Kensington Gardens by herself if she promised to go down Lanchester Terrace, and to look right, left, and right again at the crossings. She did this religiously, and thought that she was really much better at crossing than Miss Pink was, who hesitated, waited too long, darted, and then arrived breathless at the other side. "Just like a moorhen," William said once when she wasn't listening, and now Penelope always thought of Miss Pink when she saw the moorhens scurrying in and out of the chestnut tree roots alongside the Serpentine.

Lanchester Terrace was a lovely street and she never tired of it. Mrs. Prewitt said she could remember when they used to come up from Seventrees in the old days and it had been very grand—carriages and all sorts. Every single house in it was different, all set back from the road in their own gardens, some with sweeping lawns and pillared doors and some mysteriously hiding themselves behind high creepered walls. A lot of them had long glass corridors leading up to their front doors, which puzzled Penelope until Mrs. Prewitt told her that was to save the people's party dresses from the rain when they stepped out of the carriages.

" And red carpets too, they used to lay down," she said. " Them was the days."

The two best places of all were what Penelope called Mermaid Palace and Mermaid Court. In Mermaid Palace a great dome made of little tiles of curved glass had been built out over the garden, heaven only knows for what purpose, but looking as though it ought to have been at the bottom of the sea ; and Mermaid Court was a high archway leading to some mews, down which some strange creeper hung and dripped like seaweed, or like curtains of green hair waving in the wind. Little mews cottages were tucked away behind it and it was full of promise of adventure.

Now, of course, many of the houses were empty, with gaping roofs and glassless windows, but really this made it better, for lots of them could be explored cautiously and Penelope had all sorts of secret places in their gardens. In fact she quite often didn't get as far as the Round Pond, although Miss Pink fondly imagined she did. It was best in spring and autumn ; in spring every garden produced some new and unexpected wonder of lilac or hawthorn or flowering almond and forgotten bulbs pushed up through the long grass. In autumn the gold leaves floated thickly down till you could walk on them and imagine it was a country path and if you half-shut your eyes and went shuffling through them, it was almost like being at Seventrees.

The next day was bright and showery alternately, and as Penelope started out for the gardens in the afternoon with Joseph, the leaves were whirling high up in the air. Every now and again a sudden gust of wind would bring a spatter of raindrops so that it was all right to put him up. It was part of the rules, somehow, that she couldn't put him up except when it was properly raining, and in fog too I could, she added rapidly, in case it turned out to be a very dry winter.

A shower spattered down on the tight cover, and oh, he was everything she had ever imagined ! The slender stem of the palm tree stretched upwards out of her hand, the burning deep-blue sky stretched overhead as the explorer strode across the uninhabited desert ; fairy acorns grew on the down-sloping branches of the palm, while a little parrot had hopped down to look at her with a friendly beady eye. She eased her grip a moment to scratch the feathered head with her forefinger, when a sudden flurry of wind snatched the umbrella out of her hand and she saw it sail up into the air and over into one of the walled gardens.

Oh, dear ! It would be ! It was the one with the locked gate. She shook at it in vain and pealed the bell. Perhaps there were people in it although it always seemed to be empty. She ran along by the wall, looking for a gap. She must get there quick, perhaps he'd be dragging in the mud or pricked by thorns. Oh, Joseph, Joseph ! The wall led round a corner by Mermaid Court without a break or gap, then suddenly Penelope realised that the bottom of the arch was made of rough stones and that if she could climb up them she could get sideways on to the wall and jump over. Slowly and difficultly, with shoes and knees and fingers scraping and rasping up the stones, she got up, stepped on to the wall and looked over.

Beneath was a narrow flower-bed full of Michael-mas daisies, and beyond it a bright green velvety lawn on which bounced Joseph, unmuddied and untorn. Without looking any further, or thinking how to get back, Penelope made a tremendous jump clear of the flower-bed and landed on her hands and knees beside him.

She smoothed him and stroked him and twirled him all round to make sure he wasn't damaged, then, as it wasn't raining any more, she folded him up, tucked him under her arm, and proceeded to explore the garden. It was quite a large one, and beautifully kept, so there must be people in the house after all, but a glance up at the windows

It was a caterpillar house

showed them all empty and broken. Then she saw a most extraordinary thing. It was a caterpillar house, as she called them, with a long glass passage leading from the gate to the front door, *and someone was living in the caterpillar!*

Penelope tiptoed up to the glass, and half-hiding behind a low bush, pressed her nose against it and looked inside. Then she gave a gasp. It was the most lovely place to live in she'd ever seen! Bright curtains were drawn back all along the sides, cream-coloured with crimson and pale-green flowers on them, and on the floor was a rich and lovely red carpet. There seemed to be white shelves all along beneath the curtains, filled with gaily-backed books, and on the top of them were every shape and size of white bowls and flowerpots, all filled with flowering plants. At the end near the front door of the house the caterpillar took a bend and widened out into a sort of square hall; at one side of this was a brightly leaping fire with an arm-chair drawn up in front of it and in the opposite corner was a couch, covered in bright shawls and rugs. A crimson velvet curtain hung over the front door. The owner was evidently out for the moment, so Penelope peered farther and farther

in.   There was even a cat !   A fat white one in
front of the fire.   The wind had blown a rift in
the clouds, a fitful sun was shining now and all
the panes of glass gleamed and shimmered and
cast lovely beams of sunset light on the books and
flowers and carpet.

Sunset !   Whatever time was it ?   Penelope
looked round for a clock and saw one ticking over
the fireplace.   Twenty past four and she was
supposed to be back at half-past !   She ran away
from the caterpillar and started looking for a way
out of the garden.

Probably the gate was only bolted on the inside,
she'd have to open it and hope they'd forgive her ;
but no, it was locked and wouldn't answer to all
her shaking.   Penelope began to get an uncom-
fortable feeling.   She looked up at the wall and
ran all round it, but over the bright mist of Michael-
mas daisies it stretched up high and forbidding
without a foothold of any sort.   How could she
ever have jumped down ?   Perhaps the owner
would come back soon, after all they'd left the fire
burning and the cat in.   Then a chill wind of
doubt blew into her mind, perhaps they weren't
nice people and would be angry ; perhaps they

weren't even real people at all, but some sort of enchanters, it was all so queer. The light was going, and Penelope started to get really frightened. She felt terribly lonely and desolate behind that high wall. There were no sounds at all but the wind, and though she put Joseph up again for company and shivered beneath his shade as she looked round, even that didn't seem to help.

In the middle of the lawn an old twisty tree stood like a dragon. Perhaps if she climbed to the top of that she'd be able to jump across to the wall. She tried, but when she got to the top branch the gap yawned wide and terrible, with the grass gleaming far below in the fading light. She sat down in the fork and started to cry, with Joseph still bobbing and shaking over her head as she sobbed.

" Goodness gracious ! Whatever's this ! " cried a voice beneath her, and with something that was half a shriek and half a sob Penelope slid down and fell at the feet of the woman who'd just opened the gate.

CHAPTER V

A Magic Umbrella ?

She found herself being led into the glass caterpillar and then sitting in the arm-chair, while the woman poked the fire to a blaze.

" There ! " she said, sitting back on her heels, " that's better. Have a chocolate biscuit ? " and she offered Penelope a silver box.

Penelope's sobs were stopping, and feeling terribly ashamed of herself she took a biscuit and looked at the woman timidly as she thanked her. The tears on her eyelashes made the room full of watery rainbows. She couldn't be an enchantress, she thought, for surely no enchantress ever looked so nice or had a dress of such a lovely blue. Her hair was dull gold and made a shining knob on the back of her neck and as she looked at Penelope her mouth curved upwards at the corners. At one side of it was a little brown mole, like a star and a crescent moon, thought Penelope, fascinated, vaguely remembering a bit of poetry she'd done with Miss Pink. The woman's eyes were as blue as her dress.

" My name's Miss Pellay," she was saying. " Now tell me what yours is and all about yourself and how you came to be sitting in my mulberry tree with your umbrella up. Do you know, when I first looked I thought a fairy must have blown into my garden and got stuck."

" Oh ! " gasped Penelope. " And I thought you must be an enchantress ! " And then they both looked at each other and started laughing.

" I'm Penelope Rose Parfitt," said Penelope, and started telling her new friend about Joseph. Only then it seemed necessary to go back a little to explain about Daddy's present and Seventrees, and before she knew where she was, because it seemed so easy, she was telling Miss Pellay everything that had ever happened to her. It all came pouring out in a flood ; how her mother had died when she was a baby so that she didn't remember her and Daddy had always been moving round to new places and adventures. How they'd lived in all sorts of queer little houses and rooms and farms, and how now he'd gone abroad to make a lot of money for Seventrees while she stayed with Uncle Everard and Miss Pink in London.

She told her about Miss Pink, and Miss Pellay's mouth twitched at one of the curving corners, then about the darling Prewitts and how nice they always smelt, and now she could tease Prewitt by calling him Sweet William, and he'd pretend to be terribly angry and come chasing her.

"... and the funny thing is, that all our names begin with P. Pink and Prewitt and Parfitt. Isn't it odd ? And I'm P.P.R.P. Penelope for Daddy, Rose for Mummy and Prudence for my great-great sampler aunt, and Miss Pink's P.G.P., so that's even more Ps. I do so want to find out what Miss Pink's other P is for, but I've asked and asked and she won't tell me. G is for Gladys, and that's the one she uses."

"And mine's Pellay!" exclaimed the woman softly, "so perhaps it means that I can be a friend of yours too."

"Oh, yes!" breathed Penelope, her eyes shining. "I never thought of that. So it does; how lovely!" And then she went on and told Miss Pellay more and more things. How sad and quiet Uncle Everard always was and how unlike Daddy, except just sometimes, and how he and Daddy had been brought up together at Seventrees, when Mrs. Prewitt was only a young girl at the lodge. And how Parfitt used to be spelt with a "y," and there was a picture half-way up the stairs of a funny old man with a beard called "Nicholas Parfytt, of Seventrees, in the county of Dorset."

"Dorset," said Miss Pellay. "I used to stay there when I was a girl and I thought it was the loveliest place in the world."

"And Parfitt means perfect," said Penelope. "Isn't that funny? Sometimes for a joke when Daddy writes to me, he calls me his perfect Rose."

"It's a lovely name," said Miss Pellay, and under her breath she quoted :

" *He was a verray parfit, gentil knight.*"

" What was that ? " asked Penelope, her ears pricking.

" It was a poem about somebody rather like your Daddy, I think. I'll read it to you one day when you come back and look at my books."

" Please," Penelope went on politely, " do you think you could tell me a little about this house ? It's so queer and lovely and the nicest place to live in I've ever seen."

Miss Pellay laughed. " Well, there's not much to tell," she said. " While I was away during the war, I heard that an old aunt of mine had died and left me a house. When I came up to look at it I found it had been bombed and the glass corridor and the garden were the only bits left. I was standing just where we are now, wondering what to do about it, when suddenly the sun shone in through the glass and I thought—I'll live here ! You can't think how nice it is ! In the summer I can open all the glass panes in the roof and the air comes pouring in, and in the winter I draw all the curtains snug round the walls and then lie in bed and watch the stars shining through the glass, while the firelight flickers down below. And all my flowers love it here and bloom as they've never bloomed before."

The air was certainly full of the most lovely smell of early hyacinths and narcissus, and some starry, waxy sort of little lilies. Penelope touched one of these with her fingertip.

"Tuberoses," said Miss Pellay. "Aren't they lovely? And so I brought all my books and furniture here and I've lived here ever since. I had a hole made for a chimney to go through so that I could have a fire, and luckily there was just enough of the old kitchen left for me to cook in." She lifted the red curtain and, opening the front door, showed Penelope a glimpse of cooking things beyond, and the dark empty passages of the old house.

"For a long time I was terribly puzzled as to what to put down on the floor, and then suddenly, in a corner of the garden shed, I found this old red carpet they used to have for parties, and, of course, it fitted exactly. And this is Scheherazade, my white cat, but she's called Sherry for short."

The cat got up and stretched and rubbed herself against Penelope's chair, and as she did so, Joseph fell down with a clatter.

"Is that Joseph?" asked Miss Pellay. "May I see?" She stretched out her hand for him, turned him round and stroked him. Then she twiddled the little gold band till it seemed to spin round by itself.

"Penelope Rose Parfitt," she said solemnly, "do you know that I believe you've got hold of a magic umbrella?"

A delicious shiver went through Penelope; perhaps she was an enchantress after all, a white one.

"Magic!" she cried. "How do you know? What can he do?"

"I've seen one before," said Miss Pellay, mysteriously. "I had one myself when I was a little girl, but it only worked once and then I lost it, and I've never seen another. It's the little gold band, there's something written on it. Well, we shall have to try and see if he really is. Shall I tell you what to do?"

Penelope nodded, beyond speech.

"Next time someone's very upset or angry with you, you must look at them very, very hard, without wavering or moving your eyes off them, and while you do it you must twiddle the gold band till it spins of itself, from left to right, like the clock goes. And then ... I shouldn't be surprised, but I won't tell you. You try it, and then we shall know if it really works. But remember, they must be *really* angry or really upset, not just cross. Now let's have the lights on," and she switched on a row of fairy lights that were strung all along the roof of the caterpillar.

" Lights ! " cried Penelope. " I'd completely forgotten the time. Oh, I really must go. Miss Pink will be back from the Library and simply furious. But can I come back again, please ? " and she picked up Joseph and ran towards the door.

" Let me come with you and explain," suggested Miss Pellay, " then she couldn't be cross."

" Oh, no, please ! " cried Penelope. " Thank you very much, but I do so want to keep you private from Miss Pink. She'd poke so. I'd much rather she was angry."

" All right," laughed Miss Pellay, " I understand that very well. Come back very soon and next time you come, undo this little latch, then if I'm not in you can come in and play in the house or garden till I'm back." She showed her a little latch that was hidden under the ivy, and watched and waved as Penelope ran down the twilight of the street.

CHAPTER VI

A Hat with Roses and Forget-me-nots

PENELOPE hurried down towards the traffic lights, thinking only of getting home quickly, and bumped into a dark figure that was coming the other way.

" Hold up now ! " said William Prewitt's gruff voice, and she happily slid her hand into his horny one.

" You're for it ! " said he, leading her across the road. " Never seen that girl in such a taking ! " He would refer to Miss Pink as " that girl " and nothing Mrs. Prewitt could ever say would stop him. " Wrong young chap in the liberry, and now you more'n an hour late—fair rainin' an' showerin' all over the house it is," and he chuckled. "Thought I'd better come and warn ye, young rascal."

Well, at any rate the row wasn't happening at the moment, not for four minutes, not for three . . . Penelope skipped along beside Prewitt, sniffing his nice tarry, tobaccoey smell. Not for one minute, not for . . . and there they were in the warm bright kitchen. Oh, dear, it was now ! Everyone seemed to be talking at once and, like a fury, Miss Pink caught hold of her hand and swept her upstairs to her room.

" I'm sorry, I'm dreadfully sorry, I didn't mean . . . Joseph blew away . . ." but it was no good. Miss Pink wasn't listening at all and the flood of words went on and on. Penelope went wooden till it should all be over. It's a pity I haven't got a sort of invisible umbrella to keep it off, she thought, and grinned to herself. This, of course, made Miss Pink even more furious and the words came still thicker and faster. An umbrella! Suddenly Miss Pellay's words came back. Nobody could ever be angrier than Miss Pink was now! She lifted up Joseph and started to twiddle the gold band; faster and faster it went and solemnly she stared at Miss Pink.

"Don't look at me like that!" cried Miss Pink. "Put that umbrella . . . put . . . Oh!"

It was happening!

The room seemed to be full of mist. Miss Pink's face was growing rounder and softer, her fair hair was stretching out into two long pigtails, while her skirts were shrinking up till two long black stockinged legs stuck out from beneath a short blue gym dress. Then it all seemed to turn into a sort of play that Penelope was watching, though she didn't quite know from where. The funny thing was that she found, as she watched, that somehow she knew what the people were thinking, as well as saying, and what was happening round about them.

The schoolgirl that had been Miss Pink turned in through the gate of a small, newly-built house. There seemed to be country all round, but rows of the little box-like houses were spreading out into it in all directions.

A man was sitting in the window and held out his hand to her as she went into a room, pushing aside some papers he'd been writing and putting a closed envelope on top of a heavy book. He drew her on to his knee.

" I've got to go away on a journey, Glad," he said, " and I want you to give this letter to your mother when she comes back. And before I go I want to tell you a story to remember while I'm away. Will you listen ? "

Then, stroking her fair plaits, he told her a strange story about a beautiful girl who was picking flowers with her companions in a meadow when the King of the Underworld suddenly opened the earth and took her down below with him in his chariot to brighten his dark realms. And how her mother, in her sorrow, looked all over the world for her, and because she was the goddess of the crops and flowers, she forbade anything to grow again until her daughter should be found. And then at last she found her, but the King of the Underworld would only let her go back for two-thirds of each year to brighten men's hearts.

". . . And she is Spring, and all the flowering and brightness of life," said Glad's father. " The

Greeks called her Persephone and the Romans Proserpine ; and I called you Persephone when you were born, but your mother called you Gladys, and Gladys you've always been. But I'd like you to remember, sometimes, that you've got another name." Then he kissed her hard, took up his hat and a suitcase, and swung out of the gate without looking back. And because the story had been beautiful and rather sad and she didn't understand what it was all about, little, bespectacled Persephone Pink burst into tears.

Her brisk, bustling mother came in a few minutes later, read the letter and clucked. (I suppose that's where Miss Pink gets it from, thought Penelope vaguely.)

" Well, good riddance," she said, after a silence. " He was no good, with all his wasting and scribbling and fancy names. Why couldn't he stick to an honest trade and make us an ordinary comfortable home ? Well, now we're alone, Glad. You and I against the world, and we'll show them how women can do without men ! " She squared her shoulders and gave a harsh sort of snort, but Glad had burst out crying again because it was all sad, and not a bit beautiful now, and as she sniffed and sobbed, the mists came whirling down again.

It seemed to be a year or two later when they lifted, and Gladys Pink was saying good-bye to her mother at the gate before she ran off to sing in the choir. It must have been Sunday evening for the road was empty and bells were ringing in the distance. There was something very alike in the two faces now, although Gladys was still a long-legged schoolgirl. Their hair was both screwed back in the same uncompromising way, the same spectacles perched on their noses, and, oh, dear, Gladys's mouth was beginning to purse up in just the same way as her mother's !

She walked sedately along the road and into the little church, for though the village was rapidly turning into an ugly little town, they still worshipped at the old church which had stood there for centuries. She knelt down to pray and then settled primly in her seat, putting all her books open at the right place, one on top of the other.

" I say, Glad," whispered the girl next to her, " I've got some real silk stockings our Mum gave me. Just look ! "

Gladys looked at them disapprovingly.

" My mother says that silk clothes are a distraction to the mind," she said, but the girl wasn't listening.

" Oh, Glad ! Just look ! The young squire and his new lady. Oh isn't she lovely ! " and the two girls looked down the aisle to where the squire's family were settling themselves in their old square pew.

And then suddenly something happened to Gladys Pink. She saw the pretty loving face of the new bride and how her young husband leant to whisper something in her ear ; she saw how the old squire touched his wife's hand and smiled underneath his moustache as he watched them, and a curious feeling filled her, as though something long hidden were wanting to burst through. Then she saw the bride's hat. It was palest pink, with roses and little blue forget-me-nots and a cloud of pale pink veiling, and under its curving brim she looked at her husband and he looked at her as though they were drinking each other and could never drink enough.

And as from far away words came into Glad's mind, ". . . and she was all the joy and flowering and brightness of life . . ." and the organ burst

The Bride

into a lovely swelling song of triumph. Gladys felt her black woollen stockings pricking her legs and with her whole heart she suddenly hated them and yearned for silken clothes and for her mother to be pretty and for her father to come back, and for someone to look at her like that, and for a hat, for a hat, for a hat. . . .

Then the mists came swirling down again, and Penelope found she was still standing and holding Joseph, while Miss Pink was talking slower and slower, like a machine that was running down.

She threw Joseph down on the bed, flung her arms round Miss Pink and hugged her.

" Oh darling Miss Pink. I truly, really am sorry, and I didn't mean it and I'll never do it again ! What a pretty blouse you've got on, I've never seen you look so nice ! "

Miss Pink stammered, then stopped, then blushed, then cautiously kissed Penelope back.

" Well, perhaps I was a little hasty," she said. " We'll say no more about it. Do you really think it's pretty, dear ? " and as she took off her spectacles to dab her eyes and patted down the collar of her blouse, Penelope thought she really looked almost pretty herself.

CHAPTER VII

William and the Puppy

"It worked! It worked! He *is* magic!" cried
Penelope, almost before she'd got inside Miss
Pellay's gate. "Oh, Miss Pink! Oh, poor Miss
Pink, I must tell you.... Her name's Persephone; isn't it beautiful? She's quite different
to-day, she's let me come here instead of going
for a Botany Walk, she's gone to see if the right
librarian's there...."

59

"Goodness gracious, did it really happen?" cried Miss Pellay, who was planting bulbs under the mulberry tree. "Come and tell me all about it from the beginning."

Penelope stood by the tree, holding Joseph, and told her everything. Miss Pellay nodded her head as she spoke.

"That's right," she said, "that's just how it happened with me. I thought he was that sort of umbrella. Dear Joseph!" and Penelope could have sworn that he preened his feathers a little as Miss Pellay gently stroked his head.

"Oh, and it was such a sad, beautiful story he told her, about the darkness and the flowers springing out of the earth—do you know it, Miss Pellay?"

"Indeed I do," said Miss Pellay, and she held out a little withered crocus corm in her hand. "And here it is all happening over again. Down into the earth it has to go for the months of winter, and then, in the spring, the earth will let it go and all over the gardens everywhere there'll be little gold and purple flames of crocuses. And that's how the old people explained it, by that lovely story."

"Oh," breathed Penelope. "Is that what it

means ? And the hat ! you really should have seen it, and you've just no idea how badly she wanted it. Somehow all of her seemed to sort of swell out towards it, like curtains being blown out through a window."

"Then she should have it," said Miss Pellay firmly, "everyone should have what they want as badly as that, sooner or later."

"Oh, I do wish she could ! " cried Penelope. "But it would look funny on her, wouldn't it ? " and she started to giggle. " I haven't told her about Persephone, you know. I had a sort of feeling it would be better to keep it private."

"Oh, much better; besides, how could you possibly explain how you knew ? " said Miss Pellay, and started saying some poetry again :

> " *O Proserpina*
> *For the flowers now, that frighted, thou let's fall*
> *From Dis's wagon! Daffodils*
> *That come before the swallow dares, and take*
> *The winds of March with beauty, violets, dim,*
> *But sweeter than the lids of Juno's eyes,*
> *Or Cytherea's breath, pale primroses . . .*
> *. . . bold oxlips and*
> *The crown imperial, lilies of all kinds . . ."*

"What was that?" asked Penelope. "It's lovely."

"That was about Persephone too. Dis was the name of the King of the Underworld."

"You do know a lot of poetry," said Penelope. "Oh, and please could we have the one about Daddy again? You said you'd find it next time I came."

"Come along in," said Miss Pellay, "we'll have some early tea so you won't be late, and look for it. Help yourself."

A dish of crumpets stood by the crackling fire and Sherry got up and rubbed herself against Penelope as she sat down. Miss Pellay got out a book from one of the shelves.

"Oh, I do love this place!" said Penelope with a great sigh of contentment, and took a large mouthful of crumpet. "I think it's the nicest house in the whole world, except Seventrees. Do you know what I call it?"

"No, dear, what?" said Miss Pellay, smiling absentmindedly as she looked through a book.

"Caterpillar Hall. That's where I told Miss Pink I was going to-day, but of course she thought it was all a pretence nonsense."

"But that's exactly the right name!" Miss

Pellay cried. " I always wanted to find one for it. I had to paint over its real name because it was so pompous. Stratheden Lodge ! Can you imagine it ! I know what we'll do : we'll paint ' Caterpillar Hall ' in little tiny letters just over the secret latch, and then only you and I will see it. Now here's the bit you wanted," and she read to Penelope in her soft and rather deep voice :

> " *A knight ther was, and that a worthy man*
> *That fro the time that he first bigan*
> *To ryden out, he loved chivalrye,*
> *Trouthe and honour, fredom and curteisye,*
> *Full werthy was he in his lordes warre*
> *At mortal batailles had he been fifteen*
> *And foughten for our feith at Tramissene . . .*
> *He never yet no vileinie ne sayde*
> *In al his lyfe, unto to maner wight*
> *He was a verray parfit gentil knight.*"

" Oh, it is like Daddy ! " exclaimed Penelope. " Who wrote it ? They're such funny hoppity, crampy sort of words, but I do like them."

" This is the man," said Miss Pellay, showing her a picture of a man in a furred hat and cloak, with a most delightful, wise and merry face.

" Geoffrey Chaucer was his name. He wrote it
hundreds of years ago when people used to go on
pilgrimages to Canterbury, which was a holy
place, and he used to watch them, and be amused
as they all went jogging along on their horses.
Your knight had probably just come back from the
Crusades, and there's a bit about his son. . . ."

She went on reading bits here and there, and as
Penelope listened and stared into the fire, she saw
them all : the knight and his gay son, singing and
fluting ; the prioress and the priests, all swaying
down the leafy lanes of Kent ; and she suddenly
felt as though she'd made a whole lot of new friends.
To-night, before she went to sleep, she'd go riding
with them.

" Oh, my golly ! " she suddenly cried, jumping
up and looking at the clock. " It's four o'clock
already, and I'm having tea with the Prewitts
because it's Miss Pink's afternoon out. Oh, dear,
I must go. If only the time didn't go so fast.
And I don't know how I can eat any more ! "

" Never mind," said Miss Pellay, " there'll be
lots and lots of afternoons and we'll do all sorts of
lovely things in them, and meet so many more
friends in these bookcases. Good night, my dear,"

and once more she let Penelope out into Lanchester Terrace.

Still in a day-dream, Penelope swung along on her white palfrey, listening to the knight's stories of his fighting in Tramissene while the honeysuckle hedges grew high on either side of them. She was nearly home when she was suddenly jerked into reality by the sounds of a high shrill yapping and shouts of boys' laughter. Running round the corner, she was just in time to see some boys teasing a little shivering white puppy in the road. They'd tied two of its feet together in a hobble and then were hitting it with a stick to try and make it run faster, and every time it fell over they kicked it up again and laughed.

" Oh, you beasts ! " she cried, and ran towards them, waving Joseph. " Leave him alone ! " But before she got there something came up the area steps like a thunderbolt and Prewitt had one boy under his arm and was spanking the other.

" Little varmints ! " he shouted, " I'll teach you what it feels like to be hit ! " and he changed his grip to spank the other boy, but, wriggling like eels, they slipped out from under his arms and ran off howling round the corner.

Prewitt knelt down to undo the knots that tied the puppy's legs, and Penelope knelt beside him. At first the little dog tried to shrink away but when he felt Penelope's hand stroking him and heard William's gruff and tender voice he knew they were friends and gave a feeble thump of his tail.

" There, little 'un, there now," murmured Prewitt, " we'll take 'ee down for a drop of milk," and as he lifted him up, Penelope saw that William's hands were shaking.

" A drop o' warm milk, Mother," he called to Mrs. Prewitt as they went down, and in a few minutes the little creature was lapping greedily in front of the fire.

" How'd it happen, Will'm ? " asked Mrs. Prewitt.

" Them little somethings ! " shouted William in a sort of knotted voice. " Don't know as how any human creature, man or child, can want to hurt another all for nothin' but sport. Just look at his poor little quarters ! " And as he looked at the patches of raw skin showing through the white hairs, his hands clenched and trembled and his kindly face went all red.

Penelope stopped watching the puppy to look at Prewitt's distressed face, and she rubbed Joseph backwards and forwards in embarrassment, agreeing so much but not knowing what to say. Then suddenly, before she knew what was happening, the walls were melting away ; there was a keen wind blowing from somewhere ; there was a smell of salt . . . Oh, but of course ! . . . William was angry ! She'd quite forgotten about Joseph ! She went on staring and rubbed harder and harder. Now he was beginning to shrink, like Miss Pink had done, now the room was going, had quite gone, now they were out of doors and a little boy was coming home from school. Penelope could see his satchel in the light of the lamps that glistened along the windy quay.

CHAPTER VIII

Captain Seamew

I<small>T</small> was Bidmouth! Penelope recognised it from
the days when they'd had lodgings there. The
sea stretched a long arm into the little town, where
all the shipping tied up for the night, making a
lovely pattern of masts and rigging against the
sky, and along the edge of this inlet the fishermen's
and sailors' cottages clustered together on the
cobbled quay. The little boy was making for the

very last house of all, which looked straight across the bay to the Channel Islands and France.

About every third house he passed had a curving bow-fronted shop window, all full of exciting things. They didn't deal in the dull necessities of daily life here, leaving that to the shops in the town, but with all the real and adventurous things like fishing-tackle and tarred rope, lobster-pots and binnacles. Everything in them was strong and rough and satisfying : the brass, the rope, and the hard-grained timber which men used to master the sea ; and they all mingled together in one exquisitely satisfying smell of tar and wood and oil and salt. Willy thrust his hands in his pockets and drank in great breaths of it as the seagulls wheeled and cried overhead.

" And he still smells of it ! " thought Penelope in delight, from her vague vantage point.

Half-way along the quay he stopped. Here a little square opened up and wandered up the hill behind into the trees of the old fort, and at the corner of this square was a shop with windows looking both ways. Willy stared, and as he stared Penelope somehow knew that it was kept by an old sea captain who lived overhead, and bought and sold all the curios that sailors brought back with them from the Seven Seas. There were birds, stuffed and beady-eyed, carved woods, Chinese and Indian and Burmese figures, boxes of little mother-of-pearl fishes ; there were tablecloths embroidered with hard, shiny, iridescent beetles' wings. Penelope could see them all and a hundred other things as Willy looked and looked.

He climbed up the steps to the front door and pushed it open. A bell rang and went on swinging to and fro until old Captain Seamew came down and held the tongue still.

" Well, Willy," he said, peering over his spectacles, " want another look ? "

" Oh, yes, sir, please, sir," cried Willy, and the captain reached into the window and set something down on the counter. It was a curiously dimpled glass bottle, stuck on a board, with a twist of tarred rope round it. Inside was a complete and perfect little sailing ship, square-rigged, and ploughing her way across a stormy bright green plaster sea, while little plaster seagulls floated along at the top of the bottle. The cork was painted a bright and shiny scarlet.

Willy gazed at it, not even daring to touch it,

Willy and Captain Seamew

and with the little ship his heart went voyaging out across the seas, to the places with the lovely names that his father used to tell him about. Nova Scotia, Noumea, the Horn—Oh, the Horn ! —the straits of Malacca, Ascenscion . . . he made landfall at them all, for Sam Prewitt had joined Her Majesty's Navy when steam was yet unknown, and had many years of voyaging round the world.

" All but a shillin', I got it now, sir," he said to Captain Seamew, " and you'll be sure'n keep it, won't you ? Perhaps I could even get it next week."

" Lord bless, you boy, I'll keep it, longer nor next week if needs be. Don't you worry," and the Captain put the ship back in the window again.

Willy proceeded happily along the quay and had only gone a little way when something black came flapping out of the darkness towards him, almost hitting him in the face. Then it bounced on the edge of the quay and whirled down towards the water.

" My hat ! " came a shout on the wind and a man came running towards him. "Just disembarked to go on leave and lost it already. Have you seen it, son ? "

" Look ! " cried Willy, peering over the edge

into the water. " It ha'nt gone in the water at all, it's stuck in that boat. I'll get'n for you ! " and he shinned down the rope that was tying the boat to the side and came back grinning, with the fine new hat under his arm.

" That's a good lad," said the man, taking the hat. " Here ! Just a minute," and he fished in his pocket and pushed something into Willy's hand. " No thanks now, I'm the one to do the thanking," and hurried on.

The little boy went over to a lamp and unclasped his hand in its light. He looked at his palm in wonder. A shilling ! He'd got it all, what it would have taken him weeks to save. No more odd jobs, no more collecting gentles for the fishermen on the pier ! He stuck the shilling in his pocket and ran back to Captain Seamew's, his boots echoing down the empty quay. But the windows were dark, and the captain had gone off to The Sailor's Return for his pint of beer and his yarn.

Never mind, thought Willy, I'll get it to-morrow, and went skipping and hopping all the way back to Sam Prewitt's cottage while the wind flustered all round him and the sea slapped against the stones of the jetty.

He burst into the bright little room, and then stopped dead. " Liz ! " he cried. " Our Liz ! What's the matter ? "

The girl who was crying with her head down on the table raised her tear-blotched face. " Oh, Will," she said, " it's come. Me chance has come. Here's a letter from Mrs. Parfitt over to Seventrees saying she'll take me on to train as lady's maid, and I'm to go to-morrow."

" Then why be 'ee crying ? " asked William, uncomprehending.

" 'Cos she's forgotten to send the fare, and she says if I don't go to-morrow she'll know I'm not coming and mother's away, fetching Dad from the hospital and there's no one else to ask and now I'll never be able to go ! " With another burst of sobbing Liz laid her head on the table again and cried as though her heart would break.

William looked at her and he couldn't bear it. He put his hand in his pocket and pulled out his carefully collected money, first the shilling and then all the sixpences and pennies he'd been saving, bit by bit, for the last year.

" Reckon that'll be enough," he said, in a queer little copy of old William Prewitt's knotted

voice, and then suddenly turned and ran upstairs.

He stood and stared out of his bedroom window
at the wide, dark emptiness of the sea, his hands
clenched in his pockets. The little ship sailed on,
past Pitcairn and St. Helena, past Tristan da
Cunha, past the Laccadives and the Azores, into the
broad path of the sun. The seagulls wheeled and
screamed above. Oh, he would be left behind !
Wait for me ! Oh, wait ! Wait ! . . .

Slowly the walls closed in round them again,
and Prewitt was stroking the puppy gently, the
anger ebbing out of his face. Penelope moved
up close against him and looked down at the boots
which such a little while ago had been the boots
of Willy, clattering down Bidmouth quay. She
wanted to say so much and knew that she couldn't
say anything, so she just sat and rubbed herself
against him while Mrs. Prewitt set the tea.

" What have we got here ? " growled Prewitt.
" A little cat as well as a little dog ? We are coming
on ! " and he pretended to scratch Penelope behind
her ear.

The door opened and Uncle Everard stood in
the doorway.

"Have you got the evening paper, Prewitt?" he asked. "My study bell doesn't seem to be working. Hallo, Penelope, having tea?"

"I'm sure I'm sorry, sir," said Prewitt, standing up. "I was just on my way to bring it when—well, bless my soul!" The puppy, feeling that his friend was moving, had left his saucer of milk and staggered across the room to Uncle Everard. He was rubbing himself against this new man's legs.

"Always did go to you, Master Everard, didn't they? Do you remember old Lurcher down to Seventrees?"

"There, old chap," said Uncle Everard, picking up the puppy. "Let's have a look at you." The dog licked his hands with a warm, pink tongue and lay back with a ridiculous expression of bliss. "Going to keep him, Prewitt, if nobody claims him?"

"Well I never thought of that, sir, but if he wouldn't be no trouble . . ."

"Of course he'll be a trouble. I never knew a puppy that wasn't, but I dare say we'll get over that. How's your daughter, Mrs. Prewitt?"

"Oh, getting along ever so nicely, thank you,

sir," said Mrs. Prewitt, and Uncle Everard took the paper and went out.

" Well, so you're stayin'," said Prewitt to the little dog, which had gone back to his milk, " and what are we going to call ye ? "

" Seamew ! " cried Penelope, and then clapped a hand over her mouth. It had come popping out before she could stop it. Prewitt turned and looked at her strangely for a minute.

" That's a queer name," he said, " reminds me o' summat, but I can't bring to mind o' what. What makes you think o' that ? "

" Oh, it's—it's like the noise he makes," said Penelope.

" Well, it's as good a daft name as any other," said Mrs. Prewitt. " Come on, lovey, eat up your tea," and she pushed a plate of hot buns towards Penelope while little Seamew went on lapping his milk.

CHAPTER IX

A Telegram for Mrs. Prewitt

As Penelope woke up the next morning and put
out a hand to see if Joseph was still safely there, she
heard the rain rattling on the windows and the wind
howling round the eaves. She wondered what
Caterpillar Hall would be like on a day like this.
It always seemed so still and bright inside, with
the sweet heavy scent of the flowers and the crackling fire, but surely to-day the wind would make

a lovely noise sweeping up and down the glassy
sides. Oh, if only it would clear up enough to go
out this afternoon !

Keeping William's story at the back of her mind,
like a treasure to be taken out and examined later,
she went through her morning ritual. She spent
a moment beneath the tossing and creaking beeches
at Seventrees, for the weather there had always
to be the same as it was here, and looked at Great-
great-aunt Prudence's sampler. Oh, but what a
queer mix up of now's she was having ! And she
found herself thinking of all the now's there had
ever been, thousands and millions of them whirling
about like tiny pin-points. It made her feel so
giddy that she stopped thinking about it and ran
downstairs to get the post, because it was the day
for Daddy's letter.

The postman had just poked the letters in
through the door and they lay on the mat all
wet and blurred. She turned them over one by
one and felt in the box. There wasn't one for
her ! Oh, Daddy ! The tears came pricking out
behind her lids and she ran upstairs again to
get his last one. She unfolded it carefully, for
the edges were beginning to tear, and read it

over and over again till the room was full of him and she could almost hear his voice telling her the things she was reading.   About Abdullah, his servant, and his pet gazelle, and his beautiful milk-white Arab pony called Soraya, and how he would come back and fetch her one day soon and they'd ride across the desert together.

The gong sounded, so she folded up the letter and went down again.   It turned out to be a dreadful morning, starting with bony herring for breakfast and going on to algebra and geometry afterwards, which she hated more than anything.   She kept on trying to think of a way of asking what had happened to Miss Pink's mother and father without seeming to know anything about them, and this made her so distracted that she couldn't do her lessons at all, and Miss Pink got more and more exasperated.

After lunch the rain was still sweeping down as though it would never stop.

"*Please* may I go out?" asked Penelope.   "I'll put on everything I've got and change it all afterwards."

"If you had on everything, Penelope," said Miss Pink, very pleased with herself, "you'd have nothing left to change into ! No, dear, it's much too rough, and this is the sort of day that brings tiles down, and branches off trees. I don't think I'll even be able to get to the library. Settle down and do those Christmas cards of yours."

Penelope sighed, and sat down at the table with her paints, but the robins ran into the holly and the stars got green instead of yellow and it all looked horrid, so she gave it up. Then she got out her writing-case and started a letter to her father. She told him all about Miss Pellay and Caterpillar Hall and then, for some reason, she found she just couldn't tell about Joseph being magic. You couldn't somehow write it down, all about Miss Pink and Prewitt, because when you came to look for words, it just wasn't there, it was only a sort of knowing, a feeling. So—" I bought an umbrella with your lovely present," she wrote. " His name's Joseph and he's very knowing," and then she made mountains and roads and umbrellas of kisses and put " Your loving Penelope." Then she picked it up again and scribbled at the end : " P.S.—Is there any magick in Persia ? Please tell me about it. I don't mean the carpet one," and shut it and sealed it with her thumb-print on a lump of turquoise-blue wax, and lots more real kisses.

She put it in the hall for the postman to take, then she had an idea to put Joseph in the stand with the umbrellas for a little. It must be very dull for them there and he would surely liven them up, so she went upstairs and fetched him. When he was settled to her satisfaction, she had a look at the grandfather clock. Oh, dear, it only said half past three, still a whole hour to tea and then the children's hour, which would probably turn out to be for babies to-day anyway, it was being such a beastly day. Uncle Everard, of course, was away at his office ; Miss Pink was asleep. She wandered down to the kitchen to talk to Mrs. Prewitt and see how Seamew was getting on.

Seamew, however, was no exception to the general dullness of the day, for having thankfully accepted his new home and circumstances he'd decided to spend to-day in sleep, to recover from his past and set himself up for the future. He thumped his tail vaguely as Penelope scratched him but never stirred out of his misty regions of dreams.

Mrs. Prewitt was rolling out pastry and cutting it out into little rounds with a wineglass.

" Oh, may I do some ? " asked Penelope, and Mrs. Prewitt gathered up all the edges and leavings and rolled them out for her. She cut them into diamonds and rounds and ships and pastry men with currant eyes, and by the time they were cooking in the oven she felt a lot better.

" Oh, it's never dull in kitchens, is it, Mrs. Prewitt darling ? I think I'll be a cook when I'm grown up. There are always such lovely smells and exciting things to do and a lovely fire to sit by."

" Well I like it well enough, lovey," said Mrs. Prewitt, " but then I don't know as I'd be dull anywhere, except if I was a fine lady with nothing to do. But how'd you like to be cleaning out fish and skinning rabbits, I wonder ? "

" Ugh ! But I don't think I'd mind even that as much as algebra and geometry, anyway. Please tell me some more about Seventrees, Pruey darling, and about Lizzie, and how you met William ? "

Mrs. Prewitt rinsed her hands under the tap and changed into a clean apron. " Well, help me wind this wool," she said, " then perhaps I will. Now wouldn't it be nice if we was all down there this afternoon, and all them copper pans gleaming along the walls ? "

" They must have been an awful lot of work to keep clean, weren't they ? " asked Penelope, winding the white skein between her thumb and fingers.

" Work ! " exclaimed Mrs. Prewitt, winding briskly. " Who minds work when it's for brightness ? What else was we put in the world for, I'd like to know, 'cept working and loving ? And loving's work too, mostly, my old mother used to say."

" Did she always live at Seventrees too ? " asked Penelope.

" No, lovey, she came down from the north part of the county, over to Somerset way, when she married my Dad. He was groom at Seventrees then, so they lived over the stables. Then when the old man died he was made coachman, and when cars came in he was made gardener. Wouldn't have no dealings with them queer new things, he always said, four feet was good enough for him. But of course he was in the lodge by then and oh, it was a lovely little place ! The old cherry tree grew up against the window so's you could lean out and pick the fruit in summer. Come to that, I suppose it's still there now."

" Was that the tree that William hid behind when he popped out and kissed you ? " said Penelope.

" Now, Miss Penelope, I never told you that ! Well, yes, it was that tree," and Mrs. Prewitt's face was all coy and dimpling. " Come to see Lizzie up at the house, he had, and she was a great friend of mine.   So she said, ' Em, I want you to meet my brother, he's come all the way from Bidmouth.' An' there he was, as shy as you make 'em, I thought, but seems I was wrong."

" And he popped out from behind the cherry tree when you came home from the market next day, and he'd been waiting there for hours and hours, and he said, ' Em Hawkins, would you keep company with me if I was to get a job nearer to ?'   And you said . . ."

The front door bell rang. " Oh, get along with you," said Mrs. Prewitt, still dimpling, " there's the post, run up and get it now, there's a love."

Penelope went up the stairs three at a time— perhaps Daddy's letter would have come after all.   She snatched up Joseph from the stand as she passed and got her letter to hand to the postman. But it was a telegraph boy after all.

" Name of Prewitt ? " he asked.   " No reply,"
and bicycled off.

" Mrs. Prewitt, Mrs. Prewitt, a telegram for
you ! " shouted Penelope, running down the stairs
again.

Mrs. Prewitt ran up to meet her, her rosy face
gone all white and crumpled looking. " Oh, lovey,
read it to me ! " she gasped.   " I've left my specs
upstairs," and she held so tightly on to the banisters
that Penelope could see the white bones shining
beneath her plump red knuckles.

Penelope shifted Joseph under her arm, put her
letter down, slit open the yellow envelope and
read : " Lovely boy and girl born 12 o'clock, all
three doing well.   Tom."

Mrs. Prewitt sat down on the bottom stair with
shaking shoulders and flung her apron over her
head.   Then, after a few seconds she looked up at
Penelope with tears streaming down her face.

" Our May has had twins," she said.   " A boy
and a little maid."

Penelope stared at her in wonder. Why ever was
she crying when there was such a light shining
out of her eyes ? Without realising what she was
doing, she twiddled Joseph round and round.

But oh, what was happening ?   It couldn't be !
Mrs. Prewitt wasn't angry, she was terribly happy,
she . . . but the familiar mist was growing thicker
and thicker, the staircase was whirling and dissolving.   Somewhere in the distance Penelope
could see two solemn faces that were coming nearer
and nearer and nearer.

CHAPTER X

They all Wanted Something

WITH foolish, unblinking eyes the two china spaniels stared out from each corner of the mantelpiece, and beneath them flickered a bright fire. In front of this was a rug made of twisted bits of black cloth, and on this stood a little girl with round apple cheeks and brown curls.

"Here's your clean pinny, love," said a comfortable voice, and for a moment Penelope thought it was Mrs. Prewitt speaking. Then she realised that it was the little girl, smiling and dimpling in front of the fire, who was Mrs. Prewitt and that the older woman must be her mother.

" Are we going to Mrs. Trevett's t'tea, Mum ? " she asked, as the starched white frills slid over her shoulders, standing out like little wings.

" That's right, dear," replied Mrs. Hawkins. " Let's do your curls now, and then we'll be going."

Little Em stood still as her mother curled each fat sausage of hair round her finger, and her eyes were bright with excitement. To go to tea at Keeper's Cottage, all through the woods with Mum, was a rare treat. Oh, and it was such a lovely shiny kind of place when you got there ! Inside their stout little boots, her feet would scarcely keep still.

" You'll do now," said her mother, and Penelope watched them put on their coats and go out into the early autumn afternoon.

It was the drive at Seventrees ! Oh, and there, by the door, its branches reaching right up to the windows, was William's cherry tree ! But William hadn't been there yet, he was only a little boy in Bidmouth. Oh, somewhere where she was hidden behind the folds of mist, Penelope pressed her hands on her forehead at all these confusing thoughts.

Mrs. Hawkins and Em were half-way down the drive when she saw them again, then they turned off through a little gate leading into the woods and went down a path that was bright and soft with autumn leaves. Her woods ! Her trees ! Penelope was nearly frantic with excitement at seeing them so close and clearly. She watched Em chasing late butterflies and searching after blackberries as she went through the clear afternoon. At the far side of the woods the path widened to a clearing and Keeper's Cottage, like an enchanted cottage in a fairy tale, stood in front of them. There was a snow-white goat tethered on the grass.

"Come in, come in, my dears !" cried Mrs. Trevett, kissing Em on both cheeks, and Penelope watched them go in and the little girl run and sit on a stool by the fire. Here she gazed round her in delight, it was like a fairy cave ! The fire flickered and winked all over the dark little room, reflecting in the bits of shiny brass and copper that hung everywhere, polished till they were like pink and golden mirrors, for Mrs. Trevett had no children, and put all her bustling energy into polishing and cleaning her cottage.

There were horse brasses hung all round the fireplace, decorated with stars and bulls and lions and horses' heads ; pots and queer-shaped pans all along the overmantel ; a long, copper warming-pan on one wall ; and gleaming brass candlesticks wherever there was room to put them. And just in front of Em's nose, on a shiny trivet by the grate, was the very pride and beauty of them all—the copper kettle !

All the other things in the room shone like moons, but this was the very sun itself ! In its round and polished sides all the other lights were repeated and the flames flickered back again like tongues of fairy light, while somehow behind them all the green gloom of the woods outside was reflected. And there, with the trees for background and the winking moons of light all round her, was her own little serious face, copper-coloured and rosy, staring back at her out of all the rich and shimmering brightness.

Oh, it was so lovely ! If only they had one at home instead of that old iron thing ! (Penelope was no longer surprised to find that she knew exactly what the little girl was thinking.) Then she could sit at home, by her own fire, and wander at will in the copper-coloured land, among those strange shimmering leaves, while Mum and Dad talked, just as she was doing now. The grown-up conversation flowed on over Em's head, while her plate was piled with scones and butter and apple cake hot from the oven. She sat and munched, staring at the curving sides of the kettle and loving it with all her heart.

Then the cottage and the autumn woods and the snatches of conversation were all caught up and dissolved together in a rosy copper mist, and the next time it lifted again, Penelope saw that they were back in the lodge. Mrs. Hawkins was just going out. It must be only the next day, for Em had on the same starched pinafore, just a little rumpled, and it still seemed to be a radiant autumn afternoon.

" Now here's a sixpence, love," Mrs. Hawkins was saying, " and if the gipsies come this way get me a row of clothes pegs. Mind now you don't give them anything else ; they'll be asking for your clothes and your boots and everything that's in the house ; wheedlin' and twistin' all round you. But just say, ' Mum says clothes pegs,

please,' and shut the door on them. Campin'
down Inger's lane, they are, babies and horses and
tents and all. But I'll not be long, love."

She went out through the drive gate and Em
ran into the garden, where she started pulling weeds,
and carrying shells to arrange in her own little bit.
Penelope watched her darting to and fro in the
warm sun, so absorbed that she never even noticed
when some people turned in at the gate. They
were the brightest, dirtiest, most exciting lot of
people Penelope had ever seen. Their sloe eyes
slanted in their shiny brown faces and they had
clothes of every colour in the world, all faded and
blended together ; yellow and lime green and
magenta, orange and dusty blue ; worn with a
most rakish elegance. On they came, women
with babies on their hips, with baskets of clothes
pegs and brushes, with bundles of heather, and
behind them came the men, equally gaudy, leading
some rough-haired ponies.

Em had seen them by now, and was staring at
them in fascination.

" Is your Mummy in, m'dearie ? " croaked an
old woman in a tartan shawl.

" Clothes pegs, please," said Em firmly, fumbling

in her pocket for the sixpence ; " she said only clothes pegs."

" Then here you are, dearie," said the old woman, and gave her a long line of gleaming white clothes pegs, all joined together at the edges so that you had to break them off one by one, like bananas. She had put down her pack to get the pegs out, and suddenly, as it gaped open, Em gave a gasp. There, in the middle of the pack, surrounded by brooms and pegs and trinkets, was a copper kettle ! It was as polished and bright as Mrs. Trevett's, with just such a spout and just such rounded sides !

She looked at the old woman for a second, then ran indoors and snatched up the big iron kettle from off the hob. She was down the steps again and thrust it into the gipsy's hand.

" Would you change ? " she asked, breathlessly. " Would you ? Our'n is bigger."

" Copper for iron ! " cried the old woman cunningly. " Oh, no, dearie, not without something else to make up its value, I couldn't."

" Go on, Mother," said a dark girl by her side. " Let her have it," and she whispered something in her ear.

Em and the Gipsies

" Well, then, just for luck, dearie, because you've got a bonny face," and taking the iron kettle in her claws, the old gipsy handed Em the shining little kettle.   Em stood and held it to her in ecstasy.

" You give back that kettle at once, you thieving old rogue ! " cried an angry voice, and there was Mrs. Hawkins coming round the gate with her umbrella raised.   " Giving a child an old, broken, good-for-nothing kettle, and taking my good one away !   Shame on you !   No more's the clothes pegs I'll be buying from you ! " and snatching up her own kettle, she plucked the copper one out of Em's arms and flung it back to the gipsies.

As it gleamed and turned and rolled over, Penelope saw the gaping hole in the bottom.   The old woman picked it up, and, tucking it under her arm, she went gabbling and muttering down the drive.   The orange and the green and the blue of the gipsies' clothes faded away in the distance and the little girl stood by the gate and watched them. Suddenly she ran forward, stretching out her arms towards the tiny bobbing gleam that the kettle still made in the sun.   Then everything slowly faded, till only her outstretched arms were left and at last they too dissolved in the mist. Then something hard seemed to loom up out of it ; there were the banisters again, and there was William, coming in at the area door, and Mrs. Prewitt running towards him, her arms outstretched with the telegram.

The rest of the evening passed in such a flurry and warm glow of excitement that Penelope didn't seem to have time to think about the kettle or anything else. Old Prewitt slapped his knees when he heard the news, kissed Mrs. Prewitt and swung Penelope off her feet. Then he went up-stairs as fast as he could to tell Uncle Everard, and Uncle Everard, who had just come in, told him to open a bottle of port, and then came down to the kitchen to drink a health to May and the twins. They gave Penelope a glass too. It seemed to flow all over her at once in a delicious warm glow, right down to her toes and fingertips, then Miss Pink came in, all flushed and pleased, with a new library book, and they gave her one too. She beamed at them all and drank it most elegantly, with her little finger raised.

Then somehow Penelope seemed to have had her supper and bath and was in bed, with the warm

G

glow still inside her and the cool smooth pillow-case under her cheek, and all the queer happenings of the last two days came rushing back into her mind again. There were two more to tell Miss Pellay about now, William and Mrs. Prewitt! And the most astonishing thing was that it could happen through happiness too. Miss Pellay hadn't known that. Perhaps Joseph was an even more special umbrella than even hers had been. She put out her hand and stroked him where he stood by her chair.

The first opening dreams of sleep began to whirl round her in the twilight land between sleeping and waking, and in and out of them ran the three children; Miss Pink wanting her hat, darling William gazing at his ship, and Mrs. Prewitt wanting . . . Penelope jerked wide awake. But they all *wanted* something! Something that they'd never got, even now. No, she was sure she'd never seen a copper kettle, or a ship in the kitchen, and as for Miss Pink, she'd certainly never had a pretty hat. Oh, if only she could get them the things they wanted! They were all such astonishingly little things really, if only, if only she could get enough money!

There was a clatter as Joseph slipped down beside the bed and suddenly Penelope sat bolt upright. She had ! She could ! She had four pounds left over from Joseph ! She would have a Christmas party and give them all what they wanted ; Miss Pellay would help. The lovely idea spread and glowed through her mind, just like the port had done, and in the dreams that came swiftly down upon her, three children ran and shouted with faces of incredible happiness. Then they changed into William and Prewy and Miss Pink, and she rode past them at full speed, sitting behind her father on a milk-white Arab steed, and waving Joseph as she went.

CHAPTER XI

Plans for a Party

THE rain had stopped when she woke the next
morning, and the whole world glittered and sparkled
as the sun shone on the wet trees and streets. She
wheedled and begged Miss Pink to let her go out
alone to the Park in the afternoon, and danced
round her until Miss Pink said she didn't know
what had come over her, but all right, she supposed
she could.

Penelope danced down the street and opened the latch of Caterpillar Hall. There was Miss Pellay, with her mouth curving upward, telling her to come in. Before she could wait to sit down it all came bursting out of her in a great flood of words, tumbling and falling over each other.

" And they were so sweet, and they wanted it so much, and all *wanted* something, and such small things really, and I've got four pounds left, and I could give it to them, and we could have a Christmas party, and oh, please, will you help me ? And Miss Pellay, Pruey wasn't angry at all you know, but only happy ; isn't that odd ? "

" I'd forgotten about that," said Miss Pellay. " Of course it could happen that way too. And there's one other way . . ." But Penelope was talking on, and didn't listen.

" And we could have it on Christmas Eve," she was saying, " and please will you come too ? There must be enough money left to get an enormous bone for Seamew. Oh, I do wish I could find out what Uncle Everard really wants. I wonder what it is ? But he never seems to get very happy or very upset, so I don't think I ever could. I don't even think I could make him angry. Oh, well, I'll just have to get him something nice."

"Of course I'll help you," said Miss Pellay. "It'll be the nicest party there's ever been ; but there's just one thing we'll have to think about."

"What's that ? " asked Penelope.

"Well, we'll really have to know each other properly now, and not just privately, or we'll never be allowed to go shopping together. I think I'd better come and call on your uncle and ask him if you can spend a day with me. Now, let's think about what we're going to get."

They sat down by the fire and Penelope stroked Sherry as they talked.

"A kettle's easy," said Miss Pellay, "and I do so agree with Mrs. Prewitt. They're the loveliest, most friendly things to have in a room. We'll find one somewhere along Royal Street, in one of those old shops, and you shall polish it up yourself till it's better even than Mrs. Trevett's. A hat's easy too . . . we'll go to my Madame Manon, only I must just have a peep at Miss Pink's face first, and you'll have to measure her head for me some-how."

"Could you go to the library—in the afternoon?" asked Penelope breathlessly. "She's nearly always there."

"Of course I could. But the ship, that's going to be the most difficult. I must think about that. Penelope, isn't it strange they all seem to want a little thing, but really it's a big thing behind it that they want, don't you see? Miss Pink thinks she wants a hat, but really she wants all the pretty happy things in life, like her father did, and that her mother wouldn't let either of them have; and William wants the sea. I wonder why he didn't go to sea?"

"Oh, Mrs. Prewitt told me that once," said Penelope. "It was because his elder brother was drowned in the race off Bidmouth Bill, and his father was always away at sea, for years at a time, and his mother said the sea shouldn't have no more men of hers. So he didn't go, but he always wanted to."

"And Mrs. Prewitt wants brightness and cleanness and everything shining and gleaming like Mrs. Trevett's cottage did. Really hers is the easiest of all because she can make it for herself wherever she goes. But the real thing she wants is a cottage of her own."

"Did you never want to be married and have a house and children?" asked Penelope curiously, because it seemed funny for such a shining sort of person as Miss Pellay to be alone.

"Well, I did meet somebody once, a long time ago, that I would have liked to live in a house with," said Miss Pellay, slowly, as though she were remembering something, "and nobody's ever seemed quite exactly right since, so I don't expect I ever will."

A bell rang down the glass passage and Penelope jumped. Somehow she never imagined that anyone came to Caterpillar Hall except Miss Pellay and herself, and she felt rather cross.

"I expect that's John, my brother," said Miss Pellay, and went to let him in.

A tall, fair man walked in through the door, and then came up to the fire, smiling at Penelope and giving Scheherazade a scratch as he passed. He looked almost as nice as Miss Pellay and Penelope suddenly didn't mind his being there at all.

"This is Penelope Rose Parfitt," said Miss Pellay, smiling, "a friend of mine."

"Parfitt?" asked John Pellay. "Any relation to Everard Parfitt? It's not a usual name."

" He's my uncle ! " cried Penelope. " Uncle Everard that I live with ! "

" Yes, of course, I knew he lived somewhere round here," said Miss Pellay's brother. " We often meet at the club. I must tell him I've met his niece."

" But isn't that just what we wanted ? " exclaimed Miss Pellay, and explained to her brother how they'd met and how they wanted to be official friends now so that they could go out together ; though of course she didn't tell him about Joseph and the party.

" I tell you what," said John Pellay. " I'm going away to-morrow for a few weeks, till after Christmas, so I shan't be seeing him, but I'll write him a line and you can take it to him this evening. How's that ? "

" Oh, lovely ! " cried Penelope, and after he had written it they all sat down and had tea together, and laughed and joked until it was time for Penelope to go.

" Miss Pink keeps on saying I must be sickening for something because I can't eat tea," she giggled. " I'm glad she can't see inside my tummy, she would be surprised ! "

As soon as she got home she went straight up to Uncle Everard's study with the note and to ask him if she could have the other four pounds. There was no answer to her knock, but the door was ajar, so she pushed it open and went in. Uncle Everard was asleep in his chair.

Penelope tiptoed over to the chair and looked at him. He looked so much younger! All the worried lines of his face were smoothed out and his usually flat hair was rumpled up like a boy's and almost curly. What was he dreaming about? A corner of his mouth twitched upward in a sudden little smile and Penelope remembered a photograph of him and Daddy when they were boys of twelve and fourteen, taken at Seventrees with all the dogs.

She stared at him, wondering how boys changed into grown-ups. Did it come all at once, one certain day, or did it happen gradually, when you weren't noticing, like buds coming into flowers or the night growing darker? As she wondered, she rubbed Joseph slowly backwards and forwards, and then, suddenly, something strange seemed to be happening. A snatch of Miss Pellay's voice came floating back to her—" There's one other way . . ." Sleep! It must be sleep! Sure enough the room was dissolving as she rubbed, the light was drawing out of the standard lamp, clear out-door daylight was streaming in.

Uncle Everard was getting up out of the chair, but he was a boy now, the boy in the photograph. A dog was leaping at his heels and he was standing by the pillars that flanked the porch at Seventrees, he was talking to someone. . . .

CHAPTER XII

"Don't Tell Me Your Name, it Would Spoil the Magic"

DADDY! It was Daddy he was talking to! Oh, how strange to see them both as boys! Everard had his hands in the pockets of his grey flannel shorts and was kicking angrily at the gravel with his boots. Then Penelope realised that they both looked dreadfully sad.

"When did he tell you, Charles?" asked Everard.

"This morning, after breakfast. I had to go to the study and thought it was just an ordinary row about shooting in Baxter's wood or something, and it was—this."

"Oh, gosh!" Everard had no words for his despair; he sat down on the steps of the porch and looked at the ground. "Leave Seventrees! We *can't*, Charles. It's ours. It's us. We're it. It's always been ours. How can we have lost so much money suddenly? I don't understand. Why didn't Father say before? Why can't we live in part of it and sell vegetables, like the Merrions do? Why can't we . . ."

"It's worse than that," said Charles. "We've got to let it or we can't live at all, or have new clothes, or go to school at Windermead, or anything. It's something to do with a lawyer who's run away, something called trust money. And we've got to pay it back; it's an affair of honour, Father says."

"Oh, gosh!" said Everard again, still kicking at the stones on the drive. "I don't understand about money, and I don't see what it's got to do with *our* honour. But there must be a way ! They *can't* take us away from here ; it's like our skin and our bones. Oh, it can't be true ! " His fingers tightened on the pillar beside him as though they were going to drag him away there and then.

" I'll work ! " said Charles, suddenly and fiercely. " I'll work and I'll work and I'll work and never stop till we've got enough to come back again and live here. Then we'll stand on this porch and we'll touch it again, and we'll remember to-day," and he put his hand against Everard's.

" And I will, too ! " cried Everard. " But if only I could work in the country ! Why can't I be a farmer or a gamekeeper or anything—only not in Uncle Henry's office in London. Oh, Charles, London ! After Seventrees ! "

They were silent a few minutes, and as Everard looked round at the beech trees, and the downs, and the bowl of the sky behind them, he felt the warm old stone of the house beneath his fingers, and somehow Penelope could feel it too. Then something horrible and tight came into his throat and started mounting behind his eyes. Charles jerked his hands out of his pockets.

" Let's do something fierce," he said. " Let's

ride so fast we can't think. Let's ride all day. Oh, there's that picnic this afternoon."

" Oh, not a picnic to-day ! " cried Everard. " Don't they know ? Can't they think ? Can't they feel ? " And because the awful and shameful tears were starting to run down his face, he jumped up and raced down the drive to the stables with Charles and the dog close behind him. As Penelope watched them, the swirling mists clouded over the bright day and the figures of the two boys and the leaping dog grew smaller and smaller in the distance till all was mist and they were lost.

The next time she saw Everard he was somewhere up on the top of the downs, and he was alone. A few fields away she could see and hear a group of people laughing and talking, with picnic baskets spread about, but Everard had wandered away to the edge of a cornfield. He stood rubbing an ear of wheat between his fingers as he stared down at the roofs of Seventrees, far below in the valley, and beyond them to the sea. Then suddenly he flung himself face down in the rough grass by the edge of the field, clutching a handful of grass in either hand and pressing his face and his body as close as he could get to the earth.

The voices of the picnickers had died away and as the warm sun beat down on his shoulders Penelope could hear the high whirring hum of the summer insects and see the gulls that floated and flashed in the air far out above the sea.

" I feel just like that, often, too," said a voice.

Everard sprang up and sat back on his heels, his hair and clothes all rumpled and full of bits of grass and clover.

" You can't ever get close enough, can you ? But you can move with it, and be part of it, and go spinning round with it, past the moon and past the sun. Often I'm frightened that I'll fall off. Are you ? "

The girl who was speaking sat facing him, with the cornfield behind her, and far away beyond her head, like the background of an old picture, the sea sparkled in the sun. Her hair was as bright as the corn, and as she looked at him her lips curled upwards in a little secret smile.

" I came with the Chetwins," she said. " I'm staying with them. I wish I lived here."

" I . . . I'm . . ." stammered Everard, staring at her, but suddenly and surprisingly she leant forward and put her hand over his mouth.

" Oh, no ! " she cried. " Don't tell me your name, it would spoil the magic. Let's never know, or have only private ones to ourselves ! Having names makes you ordinary, makes you belong to other people." She knelt up by his side and took his hand as they looked out over the edge of the downs and the golden patches of corn to the deep glitter of the sea and the pale-blue sky. A lark sang overhead and the sun beat down and down into the earth until everything smelt of thyme and of yellow vetch.

As Penelope looked at the two figures kneeling hand in hand and staring out to sea, they seemed to be enclosed in a golden circle where there was no time, nor movement, nor sound. They turned to look at each other, their eyes sparkling and dancing like the sea with the bright wonder of the day, and started to say something, both at the same time.

" Here they are ! " cried a voice, and all the gay picnickers ran across the field towards them. Still looking at each other, they faded away into a topaz mist while the shouts and laughter grew fainter and fainter till they died on the air. Then the shining of the sea was gone, the sky was dimmed,

red curtains were hanging heavily down across
it. . . .

"What was that?" said Uncle Everard, sitting
up. For just a minute his eyes still seemed to hold
that golden reflection, then he shook his head and
rubbed them and it was gone.

Penelope couldn't speak, but held out John
Pellay's note to him. Then as he read it and she
got used to his being Uncle Everard again, the
words came back to her, slow at first, then faster
and faster till she was pouring out to him all
about Miss Pellay and how she wanted to have a
Christmas party and give everyone presents and
how Miss Pellay would help her.

"Why, yes, of course, my dear," he said, " a
splendid idea. I shall look forward to it. Christmas
Eve, did you say? John Pellay's an old friend of
mine and it's very good of his sister to say she'll
help you. By all means spend a day with her.
Have you heard from your father this week?"

"No," said Penelope sadly, "I haven't. But,
oh, thank you about the party! I'll go and tell
Miss Pink," and, looking at him curiously, she
backed out of the door and ran quickly away.

It was such a different Everard she'd seen that

she felt shy of him now, and somehow she felt
she'd been in a private place—a place where she
should never have been. She wanted to apologise.
But oh, what a nice boy he'd been ! She felt terribly
sad, for there wasn't anything that he wanted that
she could give him ; not like the others. He
wanted the air and the sun and the golden girl, and
even something more beyond all those. Who
could ever give him that ?

She felt so sorry for him that a tear slid silently
down her nose and splashed on her shoe as she went
down the passage.

A Shopping Expedition

SOMEHOW she found she couldn't even tell Miss
Pellay all about Uncle Everard. " He was asleep,"
she said. " Was that the other way you meant ? "

" That was it," said Miss Pellay. " I didn't think
you'd ever manage to do it that way."

" But it wasn't really any good, because he didn't
seem to want anything like the others. At least,
I mean he did want something, but not a small

thing . . . it was everything ! A great sort of wide open space with the sun and the sea and the sky . . . Oh, I can't explain ! "

" Poor Uncle Everard ! " said Miss Pellay gently, almost to herself, " and yet, what a lovely thing to want ! "

" But I think I could get him something about the country, a book or a picture or something, don't you ? Oh, well, anyway it'll be lovely to get the others. Can't you see their faces, Miss Pellay ! Oh, please, when can we go and get the things ? "

" What about Thursday ? " said Miss Pellay. " Would Miss Pink let you come then ? "

" I'm sure she would. She lets me do anything nowadays. She spends all her time reading books and changing them, sometimes even twice a day."

" Oh, it must be a very special hat, I can see that," laughed Miss Pellay. " I'll go round to the library this very afternoon and take a peep at her, and you must measure her head with this bit of tape before Thursday. There, I suppose I really ought to go now, or I'll miss her."

The days till Thursday seemed endless and Penelope was so excited that she couldn't even make her beech-nut magic work. Prewitt said he'd swear someone had put a frog down her throat in the night, she danced about so ; and Miss Pink said, " Oh, get along do, Penelope ! " when she clasped the tape round her head and said it was a wreath of laurels.

The most difficult thing of all was to remember not to talk about the things she'd seen and she tried to make everyone tell her about them themselves, so that they could be mentioned naturally. But the extraordinary thing was that they all seemed to have forgotten them completely.

" Gipsies, love ? " said Mrs. Prewitt. " A nasty, draggly lot they was, we was never pleased to see *them* come down the lane " ; and " Seamew ! " growled William, scratching the rapidly fattening puppy under the ear. " Can't think why you wanted to call him such a daft, silly name as that."

" No, dear," said Miss Pink. " I don't remember any of the people who used to come to church, but the singing was really lovely."

" Seventrees ? " said Uncle Everard on one of the rare occasions when she managed to talk to him. " A lovely place, but needs a deal of money to keep up, I'm afraid."

At last Thursday came, and she was so excited that she even forgot that it was the day for her father's letter, and that, once more, it hadn't come. As soon as she'd had breakfast she put on her best coat and beret, and, clasping the four pound notes tight in her hand, she said good-bye to Miss Pink and whisked along Lanchester Terrace to Caterpillar Hall.

" Oh, ! " she gasped when she saw Miss Pellay, for Miss Pellay was dressed in the most lovely and elegant clothes, made of smooth amethyst-coloured cloth with silvery, cool-smelling, furs ; and a little hat made all of violets.

" I like dressing up and going out sometimes," smiled Miss Pellay, taking Penelope's hand in her smooth, grey-gloved one. " We'll go up to the corner and get a taxi. I think Madame Manon's first, don't you, as the hat will be the most expensive, then we'll know how much we've got left."

" A taxi ! " exclaimed Penelope in delight, and there was one drawing up at the curb beside them. They stepped inside and as Penelope sat close against Miss Pellay she could feel the soft fur tickling her cheek and smell a scent like spicy flowers.

"Here we are," said Miss Pellay as they stopped outside a gay little shop with a cherry and white scalloped awning. "Is Madame here?" she asked the smiling, pretty girl who let them in.

Madame came bustling in out of the back of the shop, holding out her hands in welcome.

"Ah, Mees Pellay!" she cried. "How veree sweet is that violet toque! And what can I be showing you to-day? Is it something for the little girl?" Her black eyes beamed down on Penelope.

"It's something very special and important, Madame Manon," said Miss Pellay. "We want to give a Christmas present of a hat to a friend of ours, and it's to be pink, and very becoming, and to make her feel quite different and yet something that she won't be frightened to wear."

"And could it look like spring, please?" burst out Penelope.

Madame clapped her hands and laughed. "Ah, zat will be a hat indeed!" she cried. "I see you understand what hats are for! Now, let me think. What 'ave I got?"

She dived into a drawer and took out one hat after another till the whole shop looked like a

The Hat

flower garden, with bright birds flittering among misty swathes of rainbow tulle.

" It can't really be flowers at Christmas, I'm afraid, Penelope," said Miss Pellay, holding up a little bonnet of pink velvet. " No, that wouldn't do for Miss Pink."

" What about the new ostrich, Madame ? " said the pretty girl, who was joining in with great interest, and she went away and came back with a little cap. It was made of softly curling pale-pink feather tips, with drifts of floating veil.

" That's it ! " cried Miss Pellay and Madame and Penelope all at once, and then they all looked at each other and laughed. The hat was measured and it was exactly the right size, then Penelope paid for it and it was put in folds of tissue paper in a gay little stripy box and they went out into the street again.

Penelope was dancing with excitement as Miss Pellay hailed another taxi. " It's exactly right ! " she cried. " Oh, she will look nice ! I don't know how to wait till Christmas Eve."

" It will be the most wonderful party there's ever been," said Miss Pellay. " Now for the kettle and the ship. We'll go down Royal Street, I think, because every other shop there sells old things like that and we can poke round till we find them. Then we'll have some lunch."

Royal Street was a fascinating place with wide pavements and little shops set back from them up two broad steps. On the top of the steps they all displayed things from their stock so that you walked on past old wing-chairs, curly-fronted chests of drawers shining like chestnuts, gates of twisted iron, and almost everything else you could imagine. Somewhere nearby ran the river and they occasionally caught glimpses of it shining in the sun or heard the hoarse hooting of a barge. The air was full of a fresh watery smell, mingled with the older smells of wood and polish.

There seemed to be as much brass as anyone could ever want in almost all the shops : horse brasses and candlesticks just like the ones in Mrs. Trevett's cottage, but whenever they asked for copper it was always the same story.

" All bought up in the war to make munitions, copper was . . . Very hard to come by . . . We scarcely ever see a copper kettle nowadays. . . ."

They went from shop to shop, and were beginning to get a bit anxious. Nor did they see any ships in bottles, but Miss Pellay said they wouldn't worry about that till later. At last they decided they'd have lunch, but there was one more dark little shop on a corner so they turned into it. An old man in a velvet smoking-cap with a tassel looked up from his paper.

" Don't really know what I've got myself," he said. " Just bought the place. But look round, ladies, you're welcome," and he went back to reading his paper.

Miss Pellay looked up at the shelves behind his head, feeling, she said, just like Alice in the Sheep's shop, while Penelope poked in a box full of oddments in one corner. There were old buckles and broken silver vases, photographs of old-fashioned people, in silver frames, and brass Indian bowls carved all over with little figures. As she pulled one of these out to look at the elephants on it there was a miniature landslide of metal things and something sharp and snaky stood out from among them. Surely it was the spout of a kettle !

Penelope tugged at it and out it came, scattering buckles, brooches and medals on its way. Oh, dear ! It was exactly the right shape, but it wasn't copper, it was iron or something even duller and blacker than that.

" I think we'll go and have lunch, dear," said Miss Pellay, coming away from the shelves, " and look again afterwards." Then she pounced on the kettle. " Whatever have you found there ? "

" It's the right shape," said Penelope disconsolately, " but it's only iron or something horrid."

" How much is this old thing ? " Miss Pellay asked the shopman, and to Penelope's great surprise she bought it from him for half a crown. With it wrapped in a flapping bit of brown paper they went out into the street again.

Miss Pellay's eyes were dancing. " Penelope ! I believe it's copper underneath ! " she cried. " They never made iron ones that shape. I believe someone's painted it black. Let's go in here for lunch."

They turned into a little restaurant with bay trees beside the door and red and white checked tablecloths, and when they had ordered duck and ice-cream melba, with Penelope's eyes shining, Miss Pellay took up a knife. She gave a cautious look round the room to see if anyone was watching her, then she started scratching at the kettle. She

"She thinks we're mad"

scraped and scraped at a little piece on the bottom and at last, sure enough, some black paint flaked off. But there wasn't any copper underneath, only something dull and green.

Looking round again to see that the waitress wasn't looking, Miss Pellay poured a little vinegar out of the salad bottle on to her plate, and put a spoonful of salt into it. Then she dipped the corner of a handkerchief into it and started rubbing again. Penelope stared, fascinated. At first nothing happened, then suddenly, like a gleam of sunset, something shone out with a pink glow beneath her rubbing finger.

" Copper ! " cried Miss Pellay. " I thought so ! "

" I beg your pardon, madam ? " said the waitress, taking away the vinegar and putting down the duck in an offended way. When she'd gone, Penelope and Miss Pellay looked at each other and giggled.

" She thinks we're mad," said Miss Pellay as she wrapped up the kettle in its paper again, and they set to. " That will be a nice job for you," she went on. " We'll keep it at Caterpillar Hall and clean it up a bit every day. It'll be a beauty when it's done. We were very lucky to get it so cheap, it leaves a nice lot for the ship and for something for Uncle Everard."

But alas, though it seemed to Penelope they asked in every shop in London, no one had a ship in a bottle.

" We had one only last week, but it's gone now. . . . Haven't been asked for one of those things this many a year. . . . Yes, I remember, funny old-fashioned things, but we haven't seen one for a long time."

" Never mind," said Miss Pellay, " there are still plenty of shops left, we'll try another day. Now I think we'd better go home to tea."

As they turned into another street, they passed a picture shop and Penelope tugged at Miss Pellay's arm. " Oh, look ! " she said. " Could I get that for Uncle Everard, it's exactly like the downs behind Seventrees ? "

She pointed to a picture in a white wood frame. It was all grey and green, and the downs mounted up in great rolling curves to where a coppice of wintry beech trees tossed their mane of tangled branches against the sky. A little white path led down from beneath them and away across the downs and out of the picture—to Seventrees, in the valley, thought Penelope.

" I think it would be lovely," said Miss Pellay, and they found they could buy it and still leave enough for a ship and Seamew's bone.

A little while later they spilt out of the taxi at the door of Caterpillar Hall, happy and tired.

" Oh, what a lovely day ! " said Penelope. "Thank you so much, Miss Pellay. I only just wish we'd found William's, but the others are perfect."

The bell rang again through the bright and curtained glass hall.

" Parcel Post ! " said a voice as Miss Pellay opened up, and a large parcel was dumped down inside the door.

CHAPTER XIV

Doing Up Parcels

Miss Pellay looked at the postmark. " Bidmouth ? "
she queried. " Bidmouth ? . . . Oh," and she picked
it up and brought it over to the fire. " Open it,"
she said to Penelope, and she gave her a pair of
scissors.

Penelope snipped the string by the knot, peeled
off the brown paper, then some more and some
more until after about six layers she came to a

wooden box marked "Fragile," and nailed down.

"A screwdriver," said Miss Pellay, and brought one, with which she prised up the edges for her.

Steering carefully between the jagged, naily edges of the lid, Penelope picked out some shavings and some cotton wool and then came on something hard and glassy. She picked it out carefully with both hands.

"Miss Pellay!" she cried. "It's magic! How did it come? It's the real one, the very same one. There was a crack in the flag and I'd know it anywhere."

There on the carpet in front of them the little ship voyaged on inside its bottle. The plaster waves slapped her sides and the seagulls flew overhead.

"Isn't that wonderful!" exclaimed Miss Pellay. "I never thought he'd really find it. Oh, I am glad!" and she looked in the box and fished out a letter from the bottom, which she read.

"It's from John," she explained. "He was passing through Bidmouth on his way down to Devonshire and I asked him if he'd just look and see if Captain Seamew's shop was still there, and

I told him about the ship. Of course I didn't tell him about William or how we knew, but just that I knew someone who wanted a ship like that."

" Old Captain Seamew died years ago, he says, but they still kept the name on over the shop, and would you believe it, there was the ship, still in the back of the window, all covered with dust and cobwebs. So Captain Seamew kept his word to Willy all his life. I wonder why he never managed to collect enough money to buy it again ? "

" Oh, I think he was sent away to work very soon after that. Oh, Miss Pellay," sighed Penelope. " I could almost die of happiness. Everything we wanted, and the very same ship for William, it's too good to be true, it really is."

" Well you'd better run home now, or you'll be dying of sleepiness first," smiled Miss Pellay. " I'll keep the things safe here till the party, and come back as often as you can to clean up the kettle. Good-night, dear. Hasn't it been a lovely day ? "

Penelope ran out and home through the velvet dark December night, while the frosty stars pricked out all round her.

As the day of the party came nearer and nearer, Penelope went about with her lips twitching up in a funny little smile that she couldn't stop coming, and every now and then she jumped into the air and shouted and sang. She felt as though she were full of something fizzy, like ginger ale, which never stopped bubbling. When she went out with Joseph, her feet seemed so light on the ground that she wouldn't have been in the least surprised if they'd both started flying through the air at any moment.

She told all the people at home about the party, though not, of course, about the presents, and they all thought it was a lovely idea and said they'd be delighted to come. Mrs. Prewitt said she'd see to the cakes and all, and Miss Pink said she could have it in the schoolroom with a big fire, and she'd leave it to her and Miss Pellay to decorate all by themselves. The big bundle of bitter-smelling holly had already come from the greengrocers and was standing in the passage, bright with berries and pricking at you every time you went past, and Penelope could use as much as she liked.

Tuesday passed, then Wednesday, and Thursday came with still no letter from Daddy. This gave her a little sad pain at the bottom of all her fizziness, but everyone said that the mails were all upset at Christmas, and that she'd have heard long ago if anything were wrong. She'd probably get three all together next week. Now the party was the day after to-morrow and Penelope went through the hours in a whirl of excitement, full of bright shop windows, tinsel and hollyberries all blurred together. As she lay in bed at night snatches of carols came in from the dark and frosty streets and the whole world was bright and clear with the breathless magic of waiting.

It was the very last afternoon! She didn't get out till nearly four o'clock, and ran down the dusky street to Caterpillar Hall. There she settled down to put the last bit of polish on the kettle. It glowed and shone all over now like a red October sun, and the curving spout winked back at the fire, while another Scherherazade licked herself in the gleaming side.

"There, that's done!" cried Penelope. "Now for the labels," and she got out the little box of Christmas labels she'd bought. "Mrs. Prewitt, William, Uncle Everard, Miss Pink. Miss Pellay, do you think I could put Persephone on hers?"

" No, dear, I don't really. Let her have something secret and private and lovely that nobody knows about. It gives a sort of strength. Do you know that in the old days they used to say that cities had secret names beside their ordinary ones, and that if their enemies could find them out, they'd be destroyed ? "

" Did they really ? " Something fluttered vaguely at the back of Penelope's mind as she laboriously wrote " Miss Pink " in her best capitals. She'd heard something like that before. When was it ?

" Uncle Everard says he'll be a bit late," she said. " And we're not to wait. The others are coming at four." Then it was time to get out the tissue paper they'd bought specially and the Christmas wrapping paper with its queer, varnished smell and bright holly patterns. At last they were all wrapped and tied and stacked in the corner by the door for Miss Pellay to bring to-morrow when she came, a heap of strange-shaped, bulky packages, with Seamew's bone on the top.

" Oh, how shall I live through the night and the morning till three o'clock when you come ? " cried Penelope, and then in sudden doubt : " Oh,

I do hope they'll like them ; perhaps it's awful to get their private things like that ! "

"Of course it isn't ; they'll love them," said Miss Pellay firmly. "There isn't a doubt in the world about that. And now I've got something I want to show you." She led Penelope down the length of the glass-house and opened the door behind the curtain that led into the shell of the bombed house. The air suddenly struck keen and frosty through the broken windows and somehow seemed to smell of pine needles, thought Penelope. Miss Pellay went into the room opposite the kitchen and switched on the light. Penelope stared in wonder. There stood a little Christmas tree shining like frost in the sun with shimmering tinsel and spun glass. The draught they made as they came in swayed the branches like a breeze so that the room seemed to dance with flashes of red and green and midnight blue, all misted with gold and silver. A silver bird with a ruby eye and a long silken tail rode proudly on the top and all among the fragrant dark branches winked stars and crystals of unbelievable fairy fragility.

"That's my present for you," said Miss Pellay.

" I'll bring it with me to-morrow in the taxi and then we can put the presents round it."

" It's the most lovely thing I've ever seen ! " cried Penelope. " It's like being in a fairy forest! It's like . . . Oh, darling Miss Pellay, thank you so much ! " and she rushed at her and hugged her. Then she suddenly stepped back in dismay and looked at her with round eyes of horror.

" Oh, how dreadful ! " she said. " I never thought of it, Miss Pellay. I haven't got anything for you ! "

" Bless you," laughed Miss Pellay. " Don't look so tragic ; I don't want a present, my dear. Where would I put it in Caterpillar Hall ? There isn't an inch anywhere that I haven't used up somehow with flowers or books or Scherherazade. The sort of presents I like are adventures and just look at all the exciting things that have happened since we met ! "

" I wish I could come back to-night and find out what you wanted ! " cried Penelope, still not convinced.

" I don't think that I want any sensible thing that I could get," said Miss Pellay, and her eyes looked far away. " Perhaps I'm like Uncle

Everard. So I don't expect Joseph would work at all," she added briskly. " Now run along and I'll see you to-morrow," and she led Penelope back through the bright hall out into the darkness.

CHAPTER XV

The Party on Christmas Eve

IT was now! Not another hour, not another minute, not another second, but now! Penelope stood by the leaping fire in the schoolroom and waited for Miss Pellay as the hands of the big clock ticked and creaked round to three o'clock. She thought of Great-great aunt Prudence for a second —had she ever had a now as exciting as this one?—

and as the clock started its chirring, gathering strength to strike, the front-door bell rang.

Penelope was downstairs to open the door in a flash and there was a taximan carrying the Christmas tree and Miss Pellay with her arms full of odd-shaped parcels. The tree was carried up and the parcels dumped round it, and then, as the taxi-driver went down, Miss Pellay and Penelope stood and smiled at each other.

" Look, I brought my little wireless too," said Miss Pellay, " because one does need music at parties," and she put it down in a corner and switched it on low, so that the air suddenly seemed full of bells and singing. Then she slipped off her coat.

" Oh, your lovely violet dress again ! " cried Penelope. " I'm so glad. If only Daddy could be here ! But it will be lovely to write and tell him about it. And even after to-day's over, to-morrow's Christmas and there'll be all my presents then. Oh, I've never been so happy in all my life as now, now, now, now ! " She whirled round the room to the jingling wireless, her hair flying out behind her, till she got giddy and collapsed in a heap by the fire, with bright eyes and scarlet cheeks.

" Come on," laughed Miss Pellay, " we must put up the decorations or they'll be here before we've begun. Oh, what lovely holly ! " and they pulled off one berried sprig after another and put them round the room. " There ! That's the last, and the mistletoe in the middle. Doesn't the tree look lovely in the firelight ? Let's turn out the lights and draw the curtains."

As they shut the last of the daylight out the fairy balls winked and shone, while the dark branches threw enormous flickering shadows across the ceiling.

" Now the cakes ! " cried Penelope, and by the light of the fire she whisked off a large cloth which was covering the table in the corner. " Oh, darling Pruey, just look what she's made. Oh, look ! Oh, look ! " After a careful and delighted examination of all the little mountains of sugar cakes and brandy snaps and three-cornered sandwiches, she started off on her war-dance round the room again, ending up with a sudden twirl.

" Who shall we give first ? " she asked. " I never thought of that."

" Well, Seamew first, and then I should think in the order that Joseph told you," said Miss Pellay.

"First Miss Pink's hat, then the ship, then Mrs. Prewitt, and Uncle Everard last, and that's all right because he'll be late."

"Joseph!" cried Penelope. "I forgot him!" And she ran away upstairs and came down a few minutes later hugging him. "It's really his Christmas party; he made it all. Shall I put him on the tree, do you think?"

She dug him in beside the little trunk, and as he leant up against it, his blue-green silk lost among the blue-green leaves, his beady eye made one more winking in the firelight. "I brought the beechnut husk, too," she said, and put it down carefully on the mantelpiece.

There was a knock at the door, and there, beaming and dimpling, stood Mrs. Prewitt in her best navy-blue satin with a lace collar; and William, looking very stiff in the rusty black of his best suit. Seamew came lolloping at his heels.

"Come in! Come in!" cried Penelope, dancing across to meet them. "This is Miss Pellay, my friend."

"Very pleased to meet you, ma'am," said Mrs. Prewitt. "Oh, what a beautiful tree, isn't it . . . ?" There was another knock and there stood Miss

Pink in a black silk dress, with her hair all fluffed out—and—she'd taken off her spectacles !

" This is Miss Pink, Miss Pellay," cried Penelope, dragging her across the room by her hand.

" Oh ! I—I think we met in the library, didn't we ? " said Miss Pink, blushing.

" Yes, of course we did," said Miss Pellay, smiling. " I do think that librarian is such a nice young man, don't you ? " Miss Pink blushed even deeper and tiptoed over to look at the tree.

" Shall we begin ? " whispered Penelope urgently, holding Seamew's bone behind her back. Miss Pellay nodded her head, but before Penelope could turn round Seamew had jumped up and taken the bone for himself. He trotted off to the fire with it while they all laughed.

" Miss Pink ! " said Penelope, and taking the biggest parcel in both hands she thrust it into Miss Pink's arms.

" A present ! " said Miss Pink in great surprise. " Oh, Penelope, you are a kind girl—I'd no idea——"

" Open it ! Open it ! " cried Penelope in wild excitement, and then stood speechless by Miss Pellay's side while Miss Pink undid the silver ribbon and the holly paper and the tissue paper and the striped bandbox came into sight. There was still a tape to be cut, another foam of tissue paper and then, staring and incredulous, Miss Pink lifted out the little feather cap with its drifts of veiling.

Like somebody walking in their sleep she looked as it for a minute on her hand, then slowly she turned to the mirror over the mantelpiece and put it on, while they all watched in silence. It sat as lightly as a cloud on her fair hair and her cheeks glowed pink in its reflection, and because her cheeks were pink her eyes shone bright as stars. And as she looked at all these wonders her pursed-up lips spread curving out into a smile. She turned outwards to the room and seemed to be saying something softly to herself. . . .

" And she was all the brightness . . . Oh, what am I saying ? Where did I hear that ? . . . Penelope, my dearest child, how did you . . . how could you . . ." And she held out both hands helplessly in front of her while tears of happiness sprang into her eyes.

" Miss Pink ! " cried Penelope and Miss Pellay together. " Oh, you *do* look nice ! "

" Oh, Miss ! " said Mrs. Prewitt, clasping her hands in front of her.

" Allus said she wasn't a bad-lookin' girl," chuckled William, then he jumped.

" William ! " said Penelope in his ear, and handed him a bulky parcel, shaped like a vegetable marrow.

" Well I never ! " he growled delightedly. " Me too ? What's this—a prize marrow ? Seems a bit heavy, though. Maybe it's a Sweet William in a pot," and chuckling to himself he unwrapped it slowly with his knotted brown fingers till there on his knees sailed the little ship,

His features seemed to soften and melt till, for a second, Penelope was looking again at little Willy Prewitt with his face peering in at the window of Captain Seamew's shop. Then he was old William again, but his lips were moving. . . .

" Ceylon," he was saying softly. " The Spice Islands, Formosa and the Philippines, then maybe round the Horn, all set for home and full sail across the ocean to Bidmouth Bay." He fumbled in his pocket and trumpeted his nose with a red hand-kerchief. " Oh, Miss Penelope, what a pretty little ship ! It brings the sea right into this very room, it surely does." He reached for his handkerchief and trumpeted again, while his other hand caressed the bottle which held the little ship.

" Mrs. Prewitt ! " said Penelope, in a sort of breathless whisper, it was all going so much better than she had even hoped, and handed her another knobbly parcel.

" Oh, he's that pleased ! " cried Mrs. Prewitt, holding her parcel and looking at William. " Now he'll be minded of the sea for always. Bless you, my lovey," and she turned to her own parcel.

" Now, if it isn't the very thing I always wanted ! " she exclaimed as the shining kettle gleamed out from the wrappings, and as her face crumpled with delight little Em came popping back. " Oh, I remember a kettle like this one somewhere once, and I used to look and look in it, and I thought a home could never be proper without one, and all these years I've never had one. Oh, the shining of it ! " and she held it out in the firelight. " Brings me to mind of our Mum," she said to William, " that'd be a great-grandmother now. Just think of that ! "

Everard Parfitt stood unnoticed at the door a moment and looked at the strange sight in front of him. Everyone had fallen silent and there was

*Everard Parfitt looked at the strange
sight in front of him*

no sound except the crunching of Seamew's teeth as he splintered his bone, and the flickering of the flames as they danced and leapt and reflected in the shining tree.

Old William Prewitt sat holding out a glass bottle in both hands, gazing at the little ship inside with a far-away look in his eyes. Beside him Mrs. Prewitt stood smiling and turning an old copper kettle round and round in the firelight, dimpling back at her own reflection in its gleaming side. Standing by the fire with her back to the mirror was a pretty girl in a pink hat, looking as though she'd seen . . . goodness knows what, thought Uncle Everard. Then a thought struck him and he looked again. Goodness gracious, it was that governess, Miss Pink ! Staring at them all with solemn eyes was Penelope, holding the hand of another woman whose face was in shadow.

" May I come in ? " he said.

CHAPTER XVI

A Present for Penelope

" UNCLE EVERARD ! " cried Penelope joyfully, as
she lead him across the room. " This is Miss Pellay,
and here is your present," and she pushed a square
flat parcel into his hands.

" How do you do ? . . ." started Uncle Everard,
holding out his hand, and then a most extraordinary
thing happened.

Miss Pellay's half-raised hand fell to her side

149

and she and Uncle Everard looked at each other with wide-open eyes as though there were no one else in the room. And suddenly Penelope remembered the downs by Seventrees and the sea, and a cornfield, and a face that had been too bright with sun for her to recognise.

" It was you ! " said Miss Pellay.

" Yes. Everard Parfitt," he said. " Everard Parfitt of Seventrees."

" And I am Mary Pellay," she said. " I suppose we shall have to have names at last."

Just for a moment it seemed as if time had stopped, as if the two children were still standing on the downs, as if it were then, and now, and always. Penelope stared in wonder.

" Are you . . . do you ? . . ." she began, and Miss Pellay took her hand.

" Yes, my dear, we are, we do," she smiled, and Penelope thought she'd never seen such a smile before. " Everard," she went on, " we've waited too long not to be able to say it now, haven't we ? "

" Oh, we have, we have indeed ! " cried Uncle Everard, and the great golden light of that summer afternoon was in his eyes again. " Will you marry me, Mary Pellay ? "

For a moment everyone stared at them in silence.
" Then so *that* was what you really wanted ! It
was what you both wanted ! So I have given you
a present after all ! Oh, I *am* so glad ! " cried
Penelope. " You'll be my own real aunt, and
Joseph's done it all ! " She pulled him out of the
Christmas tree pot and danced round the room
with him, catching hold of William as she went,
and pulling him after her.

" What is the child talking about ? Joseph ? . . .
What a lovely picture," said Everard, undoing his
parcel slowly, as though he were still in a dream,
and standing very close to Miss Pellay. " It might
be the downs at Seventrees. I shall love to look at
that in my study every day."

" Oh, it doesn't matter about that one now,"
said Penelope ; " to think that it was Miss Pellay ! "

" Goodness me, Miss Pink," said Uncle Everard,
blinking his eyes and looking round, " we shan't
be keeping you here very long if you wear hats
like that ! I can see that. What a lovely kettle,
Mrs. Prewitt. How will you like to have a mistress
again ? "

" Oh, sir," said Mrs. Prewitt, " it's the best thing
that could happen in the world. Just fancy you

knowing each other all those years like that. Oh, I do wish Master Charlie could be here to see us all so happy—and all Miss Penelope's doing ! There now, there's the bell ! " and she bustled out.

" Late post," she said as she came back. " A Christmas card for you, Miss Pink, and a letter from May, William."

" Oh, it's from Mr. Thorndike ! " exclaimed Miss Pink, blushing once again. " The librarian, you know."

" There, what did I tell you ? " said Uncle Everard.

" Oh look, William ! A photo of the twins, I do declare. Their very first, bless their little hearts. Oh, the loves ! Do look, sir," and Mrs. Prewitt went over to Uncle Everard and Miss Pellay to show them the two screwed-up little monkey faces in their shawls.

" Splendid ! " said Uncle Everard, looking side-ways at Miss Pellay with an amused twinkle as he spoke. " Beautiful grandchildren you've got, Pruey."

" Oh, Master Everard," said Mrs. Prewitt, bridling with pleasure.

Penelope stood with Joseph by the tree and

suddenly felt a little sad. They were all so happy and somehow she'd got left out ; they'd all forgotten about her. It was lovely of course, oh, even better than her wildest hopes, but she did wish she had someone to talk to about it. They were all lost happily in their own little worlds, even Miss Pellay. She was lost to Uncle Everard and the whole new world they were starting. If only Daddy were here ! She stood and stared at them all rather forlornly.

The bell rang again and Mrs. Prewitt went out. Penelope heard her talking to someone in the hall, then in a minute or two she came back, beaming all over her face.

" Parcel post this time," she said breathlessly. " But you've got to go and sign for a registered one, love. I've argued, but he won't let me."

" From Persia ? " cried Penelope.

" From Persia, lovey," said Mrs. Prewitt, and Penelope ran down the stairs and into the hall, not even stopping to turn on the light. She tripped over a pile of suitcases at the side of the stairs and fell headlong into someone who was standing by them.

" Well, if it isn't my prudent and perfect Rose ! "

She tripped over a pile of suitcases

said a voice, and with a little sob Penelope buried her face in a blissful, scratchy darkness of tweed while her father's arms went round her.

" I've done it, Penelope," he said after a little while. " I had a bit of luck and we can go back in the spring. Did you wonder why I didn't write ? It was because I was travelling, and I wanted it to be a Christmas surprise."

Penelope gazed at him in the dark hall with wide-open eyes. " Back to Persia ? " she asked.

" No, no—to Seventrees," he said. " Home."

" Oh, glory ! " suddenly shouted Penelope and started leaping and dancing all round him until she fell over another suitcase. " Let's go up and tell them," she cried, " and, oh, so many things have happened, Daddy. Uncle Everard's going to marry Miss Pellay and he's known her all the time, and Miss Pink's gone all pretty, and William's got grandchildren, and there's a dog called Seamew and a very magic umbrella called Joseph. . . ."

" Goodness gracious," said her father, who was being led upstairs while all this went on. " I shan't know where to begin ! Everard ! My dear chap, what's all this I hear ! William ! I hear you're a grandfather. Mrs. Prewitt ! And this must be Miss Pink." Then he stopped in front of Miss Pellay and held both her hands. " And this ? " he said.

" Your future sister-in-law, I'm afraid. Will you mind ? " Her mouth curved upwards as she looked at him.

" Would *you* mind, I wonder, living at Seventrees ? " he said. " Because I don't think I could bear it without old Everard when we move there in the spring. The lodge'll be ready for you, Mrs. Prewitt. And what about you, Miss Pink ? No need to ask you, old fellow," and he tickled Seamew in the ribs.

" Seventrees ! " said Everard. " Is it really true ? "

" It's as true as can be," said Charles. " And we'll stand by the porch and touch the stone together as we always said we would. Do you remember ? "

" And find all our secret marks too ! " cried Penelope. " And put our beech-husk back," and she joined hers from the mantelpiece to the one her father held out.

" I always wished I lived there," said Mary Pellay.

" That dear little cottage—and our cherry tree, Will ! " cried Mrs. Prewitt. " And we could have May and the twins down to stay, often."

" Seventrees ! " growled William, " with the sea only a mile or two away and the sniff of it coming up over the downs ! "

" I—I should love to come," said Miss Pink. " But it's just possible that I might have other plans."

Seamew left his bone a moment to lick Daddy's shoe. Penelope said nothing, then suddenly a thought came to her and she tugged at Miss Pellay's arm.

" They've all got *both* things ! " she whispered excitedly. " Oh, don't you see ! We gave them the small things and now the big things have come by themselves ! "

" So they have," whispered back Miss Pellay. " Oh, dear Joseph ! And I tell you what," she said, bending down and whispering even more softly, " we'll keep Caterpillar Hall for our town house, just you and me."

They all stood and stared at each other in the delight of their thoughts, when suddenly in the silence a boy's voice rose from the wireless they'd all forgotten. Like a bird with silver wings it soared and fell and soared again :

> " *Of His love and mercy mild*
> *This the Christmas story.*"

Then, as the mighty chords came rumbling out of the organ, Everard and Charles ; William's cracked bass and Mrs. Prewitt's trembling soprano ; Miss Pink, surprisingly sweet and true ; Miss Pellay's husky velvet and Penelope's triumphant shout all joined and swelled in the chorus together :

> " *O and A, and A and O!*
> *Cum cantibus in choro,*
> *Let the merry organ go*
> *Benedicamus Do o o o o o o min o.*"

Seamew lifted his head and howled a little in sympathy, then he went back again to the juicy marrow of his bone.

THE END